SUNDAY SAINTS

By: Stepfun

Acknowledgments

First, honor goes to God for the gift and for allowing this book to come to fruition. I've been writing all my life, and this story is among several that had been tucked away in my closet for many years.

I am grateful to all of my family and friends who have encouraged and supported me in my writing journey.

I am especially grateful to Lori for typing my manuscript, to Jen for being my first reader and encouraging me to publish my story, and to Edna for reading my story 15 years later and assuring me that it is still relevant and needs to be shared.

Dedication

To Ma Mert, Ma Bessie, Aunt Irene and Chris. I wish you were here in person for this experience. But, even though you aren't, I know that you are with me in spirit. I love and miss you all, and I dedicate this book to you.

Scripture

So that no one can criticize you. Live clean, innocent lives as children of God, shining like bright lights in a world full of crooked and perverse people.

Phillipians 2:15 (NLT)

Table of Contents

Sunday Service

WE SING THE PRAISES TO THE KING

FOR HE IS THE KING OF KINGS

WE SING THE PRAISES TO THE KING

FOR HE'S THE KING OF KINGS...

The choir sings as the congregation rejoices while dancing and clapping to the uplifting rhythms being produced by the combination of the organ, piano and drums.

"COME ON AND GIVE HIM GLORY, " Pipes the lead songstress, after which the choir follows her lead with "FOR HE IS THE KING OF KINGS….".

As the song continues, the presence of God can be felt all over the building. A lady wearing a peach-colored hat begins to shout. The ushers surround her just in time enough to save her from falling flat on the floor, but not in time enough to catch her hat which goes flying across the room, landing directly on the head of Cleotis James just as he was about to doze off. It startles him, and he reaches up quickly to grab at whatever has just hit him in the head and interrupted what would have been at least 10 minutes of good, undisturbed sleep. He knows that the only way anybody pays attention to you during praise and worship is if you are shouting. He takes a quick glance in his wife's direction, trying to avoid direct eye contact, but despite his best effort, their eyes meet. She disapprovingly rolls her eyes at him. "Dang it!" He thinks to himself, "The old hen was watching. I'll never hear the end of it." He looks over at his wife again to see if she's still watching. To his surprise, he finds her slain by the spirit and sprawled out on the floor. The ushers rush to her side with their fans, body covers, and smelling salts.

The music starts to fade as praise and worship come to an end. As the music stops, so does the shouting and the praise. Like clockwork, people return to their seats and look toward the altar, waiting to see what will happen next. The young Rev. Magee, Judah Temple's very handsome and overly confident Co-Pastor, approaches the podium. Rev. Magee is wearing his new Armani suit, and he knows that he is, without a doubt, looking good today. It was no secret that many of the women in the church, both young and old, were awed by his good looks. "AINT GOD GOOD!" Rev. Magee loudly exclaims as he strides past the podium and descends the steps from the pulpit into the congregation. Halfway down, he starts jumping in place. The music starts back up again, and so does the praise. People start dancing and shouting all over again to the sound of the music.

When the music stops again, Rev. Magee makes his way back up into the pulpit. Hallelujahs and amens can be heard all throughout the congregation. "Ya'll be seated," he says as he walks over to the podium and goes to stand behind it so that he can continue on with the order of service. Rev. Magee knew how important sticking to the order of service was at Judah's Temple. The church leaders, many of whom had been members of Judah's Temple since its practical beginnings, frowned on deviating from the order of service. He didn't want to give any of the church leaders a reason to be disgruntled with him. He intended to be the Pastor of Judah's Temple one day, just as his grandfather and great-grandfather had been. He had decided that until then, he'd just play the game that would allow him to stay on everyone's good side. Right now, as Co-Pastor, he was second in command to his long-time best friend and fraternity brother. The two were inseparable. Each trusted the other with his life. Not only had they been through a lot together, but they also shared some pretty significant secrets that no one else knew about. For Rev. Magee, having his best friend be the Pastor was like the next best thing to being the Pastor himself.

"Give the Lord a hand praise," instructs Rev. Magee. Everyone claps. Praises ring throughout the congregation. "Amen," Rev. Magee continues on in a much more somber and business-like voice. "Now we will have the reading of our announcements by Sis. Sally James….praise God."

Sis. Sally James goes to the microphone, looking very proud and important with her stack of announcement papers. Sis Sally James had been delivering the announcements for over 20 years. It was her position. Everyone at Judah's Temple knew it and no one dared to try and replace her. Sis. Sally James was very direct and could be quite intimidating. She had the looks and demeanor of a mean old schoolteacher, the kind who would give you a lick or two for crossing her. Before she begins,

3

she puts on her glasses, looking over the top of them as if to do a quick once over of the audience. She then looks down to begin reading the first of the announcements. 'The members at Judah's Temple would like to welcome all of our visitors. Visitors, would you please stand." She pauses just long enough to allow for all the visitors to be acknowledged.

"We'd also like to remind you to continue to donate to our building fund. These are your announcements, please govern yourself accordingly. Thank you." Upon completing her presentation, Sis. Sally James saunters back to her front row pew, looking very smug and obviously proud of how her announcements had gone. As she takes her seat, she peers over at her husband Cleotis to see if he had managed to stay awake for her announcements. "Looks like the old drunken heathen did manage to stay awake this time," she thinks to herself and raises her hand just in time to exclaim hallelujah to whatever it was that the Rev. had just said.

Cleotis notices her looking in his direction and is glad that she has caught him with his eyes wide open. If she had suspected that he was sleeping during her announcements, he would never have heard the end of it once they left church that day.

After the offering is collected, the honorable Pastor Parish takes his place at the podium to deliver the sermon for the day. Rev. Magee is eager to turn over the microphone to his good friend for the remainder of the service. His mind is on the gorgeous visitor that had caught his eye earlier. "Fresh game, I've got to get me some of that!" he thinks to himself as he glances in her direction to take another look.

The soul-stirring sermon is phenomenal, and afterwards, there is standing room only at the altar. At the end of service, Pastor Parish rushes to the door of the sanctuary to greet his parishioners and visitors just as he had done since his very first day as Pastor of the church. Rev. Magee also rushes to the door and stands by Pastor Parish's side greeting the congregation as they leave. Pastor Parish notices his friend and gives him a quick 'What's up with you' look before diverting his attention back to his people. Rev. Magee responds to Pastor Parish's unspoken inquisition with a wink. He then turns to notice the visitor of interest fast approaching. He reaches to grab a visitor's card. He wants to make sure that she doesn't leave without filling one out. He planned to call her with a personal invitation to come back, and to let her know that he would keep her in his prayers. Indeed, he would. He could tell that underneath that conservative church girl dress she wore, she was hot, and he was going to be praying for *'revealation'.*

Cussing Christians

"Did you see what that floozy had on at church today? That don't make no damn sense. Hell, her mama must didn't teach her ass nothing, and now she got all those damn kids….what can she teach them?"

"What did you say, dear?" was Deacon Douglass's innocent reply. He knew full well who she was referring to. He just didn't want to give her the satisfaction of knowing that he'd noticed because that would have opened up a whole other can of worms. It would have given them something to argue about, and Deacon Douglass didn't feel like it today. If she knew that he had noticed, she would accuse him of lusting after other women in the church house and spend the whole day cursing him out. All he had on his mind today was the football game, and if he played his cards right, he'd be able to enjoy it peacefully.

"I'm talking about that whore Demetria," Sis. Be Be replies sharply, "With her ghetto ass…..coming up in the church in that tight ass dress with all her cleavage hanging out. It's a damn shame. Somebody ought to tell her about herself."

Kiara sits quietly in the backseat of their BMW and stares out the window. She tries to ignore her mother's ranting and raving. Her mother was always ranting and raving about one thing or another that was really no big deal. Besides, she saw nothing wrong with what the lady had worn. "That dress was sexy," she thinks to herself, "and if you got it, you may as well flaunt it." She figured her mother was probably just jealous that she didn't have it…..at least not anymore. She'd seen old pictures of her mother and was aware that her mother had been very beautiful once upon a time. In fact, she herself looked like the split image of the pictures that she had seen of her mother at age sixteen. But now, her mother just looked like any other mom. Not bad, just motherly.

Deacon Douglass chose his words carefully, "Well baby, you are over the women's auxiliary committee, and she is a junior member……maybe you could pull her to the side privately one day and talk to her about it." His wife did not respond. "I got her with that," he thought as he chuckled to himself, "I knew that would shut her up." His wife could talk about people behind their backs all day long, but he knew that no matter how much Sis. Demetria's clothes bothered her, and she didn't have enough backbone to confront her. And even if Sis. Demetria did start to dress more conservatively, but that would only have given her less to gossip and complain about, and in that case, whatever would she find to do with all the free time she had on her hands then.

Moments of silence pass by, and finally, she responds. "I ain't got nothing to say to that stank ass whore, hell, she's a grown ass woman with a bunch of kids. She should already know better."

Deacon Douglass shakes his head and reaches to turn up the volume on the radio. He pretends to be interested in the song that had just come on. His wife sits tight lipped and as quiet as a church mouse the rest of the way home.

Secrets

"Hello, can I speak to Rossi," Kiara says into the phone, making an effort to sound as grown up as possible.

"Just a minute," responds the shaky and tired voice on the other end of the line. Rossi's seventy-five-year-old mother had answered.

Rossi, better known as Bro. Ross, at Judah's Temple, was the church's lead musician. He was extremely talented but also very suave and debonair. He was twice Kiara's age, but he had a thing for perky little teen-aged girls. Bro. Ross was fine and always dressed to a 'T'. All the young girls in the church choir flirted with him, but in Kiara's mind she was the only one. He was hers, and she didn't mind doing what she had to do to keep it that way…even if it did mean keeping their relationship a secret. Rossi had warned her several times about all the things that could happen to destroy their relationship if anyone ever found out about them. Kiara was always extra careful about being discreet, even though sometimes it made her really mad to see other girls in the church practically throwing themselves at her man. Sometimes it looked to her as though Rossi enjoyed it, but he always reassured her that it was just part of his strategy to keep people from being suspicious about their relationship and that she was the only one he really loved. Rossi always knew just the right words to say to make her feel better. One thing that Kiara knew for sure was that her parents could never find out about their relationship. Her parents were very well respected in the church and community. If they ever found out what she was doing, she was certain that she'd be disowned for ruining their family's good name.

"Hello," exclaimed the gruff, sleepy voice on the other end of the phone.

"Hello, it's me, Kiara."

"Oh hey, sweet thing."

"So, what you wanna do?"

"About what, baby?"

"About tonight. I thought you said you wanted to spend some time together. Are we going to a hotel or what?"

"It's all on you baby, you gone be able to break out tonight."

"Yeah, I'll just pretend I'm going to bed early. They won't bother me after that. I'll just lock my room door and sneak out the window."

"Look at you, girl. You got it all worked out, huh?"

"Yep."

"All right then, baby girl. Well, come on with the come on. I don't want no mess now, cause you know it's gone be on tonight. You ready for big daddy?"

"Yep." Kiara giggled.

"OK, then. I'll pick you up around 9:00 at the usual place, alright?"

"Alright."

"OK. So, go handle yo' business, my little love.

Click. Kiara places the phone gently back on the receiver so as to keep anyone else from hearing. She'd convinced her dad to let her have her own personal line installed for her 16th birthday and she knew that no one else was listening, but she always felt as though she had to be extra careful on the phone. She didn't even like to think about what would happen if her parents ever found out about her and Rossi. She didn't really care so much about what they'd do to her. Her concern was for Rossi. She loved him so much and she feared what they would do to him. She couldn't live without him. Nobody understood her, or cared for her like he did. He treated her like somebody special, and he knew how to make her feel so good. Rossi always made time just to be with her, and she liked that. She had to protect him, even if it meant lying to her parents. They were always so busy working at the church and all. They never made time for her like Rossi did. In her mind, she was just getting the love that she deserved. Since her parents never had time for her, why should they care? Nevertheless, she knew that she still had to be careful. So, she was always very cautious about covering her tracks when she was going to be with Rossi.

Kiara had been secretly seeing Rossi for almost six months. She would sneak out her bedroom window and walk about two blocks from her home. Rossi would always be waiting for her there. He'd always drive his mother's car when he was going to be meeting with Kiara. His mother had been unable to drive it herself since her stroke two years ago. No one in the area knew his mother's car. He couldn't afford to risk having someone see Kiara getting into his. They'd drive about 30 minutes away to a hotel, and they would frequent a different one each time. They didn't want anyone to become too familiar with them.

Kiara turns on her TV and sits on her bed, half focused on the Buster Rhymes video that was showing on the screen. She looks up at the clock often, awaiting what she thinks will be the right time to inform her parents that she will be going to bed early. Finally, the sun goes down. Kiara showers, and then wraps herself in her warm and fluffy bathrobe. "Now is as good a time as any," she says to herself and then sticks her head out her bedroom door just far enough to yell down the hall for her parent's attention. "Good night mommy and daddy. I'm tired. I'm going to bed early tonight. I'll see you in the morning. I love you!"

"Good night," they both yelled back in almost perfect unison.

Kiara closes her room door and carefully checks to make sure that it locks before slipping into a pair of jeans and a tank top. She grabs her purse, checking inside to make sure that she has the birth control sponge that she'd purchased at the drug store yesterday, slips her sandals on, and makes her quiet escape out the bedroom window.

A Little Peace of Mind

Cleotis undresses quickly, changing from his well pressed slacks, shirt, and tie into a pair of loose-fitting casual slacks and a comfortable pullover shirt. Against his own wishes, he had gone visiting the sick and shut in with Sally today after church. They had stopped to get a bite to eat afterwards and were just now making it home. He would rather had just come home after the service and relax, because in a few hours, he'd have to leave for his part-time job at the motel. But Sally always made such a fuss about his lying around doing nothing while she was out doing the Lord's work. Sally was a faithful church worker. In fact, since she'd retired from teaching five years ago, and now she spent most of her time doing one thing or another for the church. Cleotis never would have told her so, but he often felt as though his wife thought that the church revolved around her. Sally was highly respected in the church, and she thrived on that respect and all the recognition that came with it.

The game would be starting soon, and Cleotis didn't want to miss a second of it. He had just enough time to grab some pork rinds and a beer from the fridge before settling into his favorite chair, an old worn-out lazy boy that Sally kept threatening to throw out.

He was surprised that the old hag had only threatened up until now. It seemed, sometimes, like her mission in life was to make him miserable. Most of the time, she succeeded.

It was no secret that Cleotis had a drinking problem. Everyone around town knew it.

This embarrassed and irked Sally because she felt as though his drinking problem was a direct reflection on her, and that it somehow affected her good name. She never let the opportunity to remind Cleotis of what a drunken embarrassment he was slip by. Holding this over his head somehow made her feel like she was a level above him, and for the last 20 years, she had put a lot of time and effort into trying to change him so that he could do things the right way.... or, at least her way. There had been several times when Cleotis had thought about packing his bags and leaving her, but he never had. He had been with Sally for so long that he had grown used to her and all of her 'better than thou' antics. He'd come to the conclusion that it would be far less trouble and inconvenience to simply keep ignoring her, just as he had become accustomed to doing for so long now. When the pressure got to be too much, he'd just bury himself in a bottle. At least then for a little while, everything would be alright.

Cleotis settles into his seat and clicks on the TV just as the kickoff begins. "Alright, Cowboys, show me something, now. I got money riding on this game, and I needs my money." Cleotis grumbles while cramming a handful of pork rinds into his mouth. He looked around to make sure that Sally hadn't entered the room and overheard what he'd just said. She would never stand for gambling.

Hidden Motives

"Hello, may I speak to Miss Ciara Porter?"

13

"This is she."

"Hi, yes, this is Rev.Julius Magee, the Co-Pastor at Judah's Temple. I'm calling on behalf of our welcome committee."

"Hello Rev. Magee. I must say, it seems a little weird that the Co-Pastor at a church as big as Judah's Temple would have to be on the welcome committee. It's also very surprising to hear from your church so soon."

"Well, you know Sista, I like to stay in the trenches and help out where I can. I had some free time on my hands today, so I decided to stay over after church to catch up on some work and make a few calls. Nothing wrong with that, is there?" Rev. Magee listens closely and tries to read her reaction through her voice. He didn't want to give her any reason to be suspicious. That would mess up his plans.

"No, not at all Rev. Magee. I appreciate your call. Is there anything else?"

"I just wanted to let you know that we appreciated your visit today. We realize that you could have chosen to worship anywhere, but you chose to come worship with us. We don't take that lightly. Did you enjoy the service?"

"Yes, I enjoyed it very much."

"Good, then I hope that you and your family will come again. You are welcome back anytime." Rev. Magee hadn't noticed anyone else with her and he'd checked. He also didn't notice a ring on her finger.

"Oh, I don't have family here. It's just me and my 2-year-old son. We recently moved here from Florida."

"Bingo," thought Rev. Magee, "no husband in the way to complicate things." He spoke again, "Well, my sister, I don't want to hold you up. I just wanted to let you know that I, I mean we at Judah's Temple were thinking about you and that we will be praying for you. If you are ever in need of anything, feel free to give us a call. You can call our church directory which will connect you with any one of our prayer warriors, including myself. OK?"

"Ok. Thank you so much for calling Rev. Magee. You have really made me feel welcomed."

"You are welcome, and I hope to see you soon, Ok." The Rev. Magee thought to himself as he hung up the phone, "If she lets me, I plan to make her feel so much more."

"I hope to see you again real soon," he says out loud as he leans back in his chair just far enough to kick his heels up and land them on top of his desk. "Real soon," he thought before he hung up the phone.

Power in the Word

As night falls, Pastor Parish sits meditating at his desk and thinking back over the message that he had delivered during the church service earlier this afternoon. It was his custom to do so late on Sunday evenings, just as it was also his custom to start preparing his sermon for the next week. His wife Simone walked up behind him and gently caressed his shoulders. "That was one powerful message you delivered today, Pastor," she said. She bent over to kiss him softly on the cheek. Pastor Parish, enjoying the enticing scent that his wife is wearing, and her soft touch, stops what he is doing and turns toward his wife. He is about to respond to what she has just said but is immediately caught off guard and aroused by what Simone is wearing and how beautiful she looks. Simone was wearing a red silk negligee that she had just purchased from Victoria's Secret and matching red pumps with a spiked heel. She steps back, places her hands on her hips, and does a half turn to give her husband a better look.

"I am married to the most beautiful, hot, and sexy woman in the world," says Pastor Parish, smiling like a kid in a candy store.

"You like?" asks Simone as strikes several sexy poses.

Simone had given birth to two children but had managed to keep almost the same perfect figure that she had prior to her pregnancies. She was, of course, a little fuller now in certain areas than she had been previously, but she had embraced her bodily changes, feeling blessed that all her extras had somehow managed to settle in just the right places. She was pleased with her body. She was even more pleased with how much her husband loved her body.

Pastor stares dreamingly at his beautiful wife. She has made him forget all about his sermon. All he can think about now is how much he wants her. He reaches his hand out to her. Simone stops posing, strolls toward her husband

and sits straddling his lap. She kisses him gently on his nose. He feels himself becoming more and more aroused.

"You know," she says in a soft, sexy voice, "there's a lot to be learned from the word that God spoke through you today. You said some really good things that a lot of our congregation really needed to hear."

"Um hum," he replies, trying to control what he is feeling.

"As a matter of fact, you said a lot of good things that I needed to hear too," she says before landing a kiss on his neck. "I was really blessed by that sermon as well."

Oh yeah, and just what did you get from the sermon, my Angel?" says Pastor, trying hard to ignore how turned on he is right now and focus on what his wife was saying.

"Well, I learned that you can't run from your destiny," Simone continues to tease, now placing a soft kiss on her husband's strong and muscular chest.

By now, Pastor Parish is hardly able to control himself. His heart is racing, and he is now breathing hard. His hands start to explore his wife's body.

"And how does that apply to you?" he manages before he begins to kiss his wife uncontrollably on her neck and shoulders. His passionate kisses cause Simone to become very aroused also.

She can hardly keep still at this point. She begins to squirm, her body moving almost automatically in a back-

and-forward motion against her husband's smooth and firm body, but she continues talking.

"I've come to realize that my destiny is in God's hands, and that what He has for me is already mine. I also heard you say that God knows our every move...." She kisses his lips softly.

"He knows my every thought....." She kisses him behind the ear.

"And my every desire," she kisses his shoulders and seductively moves on to tease his chest with her lips and tongue.

"He knew I was gonna do that," she whispers softly in his ear. She begins to move her hands up and down his anxious body and undresses him slowly.

"And you know what else......He knows that I am destined to do what I'm about to do to you."

The Order of Business

"This meeting is now called to order."

Everyone in the room grows quiet and begins to focus their attention on the front of the sanctuary where Pastor Parish and Deacon Douglass are seated. Deacon Douglass begins. "The first order of business is the building fund. Some of our members seemed to have slacked off on paying their building fund dues. We've come up about two thousand dollars shorter than projected for this year. Last I heard, y'all say you wanted to try and add the new wing on by the end of the year. Everybody said they were gonna be faithful in their contributions, but we keep coming up short and this is a problem. We just can't get people to commit like they ought to and follow through. People just won't do what they say they gone do."

"Excuse me Deacon, but what did you say that amount was again?" asks Pastor Parish, hoping to divert the Deacon's and everyone else's attention away from the tangent that he knew would soon begin if he didn't say something. Discussions about money always led to heated arguments between the board members.

"Two thousand dollars, Pastor. I'm sorry, I didn't say that loud enough, its two thousand dollars short."

"Thank you, Deacon," Pastor Parish's ploy had worked. "And how much do we currently have in our building fund?"

"Well, let me see here…" Deacon said, thumbing through the papers before him. "We currently have about $247, 672.50. We should have ended the year with almost $250, 000.00.

"I see, and have we used any of the building funds for other renovations? Is it possible that we might have spent more than we budgeted for on any of those projects?"

"Pastor, I say the problem is that folks just won't do what they say they gonna do, but I'll check with accounting this week to get a better idea of just what happened."

"Thank you, Deacon Douglass, I'd appreciate it if you did that, and you can get back to us with that information at our next meeting. Now then, what's our next matter of concern?" Pastor Parish was pleased at how he had diverted the situation.

No one spoke, but Pastor Parish could sense the uneasy atmosphere in the room. He also sensed some disturbance among the older members of the board. He was certain that they weren't happy about his abrupt interruption of what would have turned out to be an all-evening gripe session had he not interrupted. The building fund was considered of high importance to the old board members, even though it hadn't been used to build anything in the last 10 years. He was sure that he'd hear from some of them about it later. He'd grown accustomed to hearing about how the honorable Rev. Magee would never have done this, that, and the other. He'd deal with that when he had to, but as for now they'd go on with the business at hand. If he didn't take control of the meeting and direct them to focus elsewhere there would be arguing, tempers would flare, feelings would be hurt, and no real solutions for any of the church issues that really mattered would be addressed. As far as Pastor Parish was concerned, this had happened far too many times already.

"I HAVE A CONCERN." The silence was broken by Sis Sallie James who was well known for being a little too loud and a little too outspoken at times. "I am concerned about the management of our poor plate collection funds." Relieved that the silence had been broken, Pastor Parish turned his attention to Sis. Sally James.

She stood. "I am concerned that the money we take up in poor plate collections is not being handled right. It seems to me like we're giving to the same people all the time, and those same people don't never give nothing back. They come to church all the time with fancy clothes on, and they got their hair and nails all done up, but when it comes time to give, they aint never got nothing. No tithes, no offering, nothing! But they all the time needing and getting. Now, I say we need to use more discretion about who we're giving our money to."

"Amen," someone in the back of the church agreed. Sis Be Be glanced approvingly at Sis Sally as she nodded her head in agreement. "The Old Biddie," she thought to herself, "she finally said something that made some sense." The two women never agreed on much, but Sis Be Be knew that she was referring to that sleazy Demetria Thomas. "All them kids and not a daddy to show for neither one of them," she mumbled under her breath.

"Was that all you had to say, Mrs. James," Parish asked with a look of concern on his face.

"Yes, that was all," was her smug reply. She returned to her seat looking very satisfied with herself.

"Thank you, Mrs. James, for your comment and concern." Replied Pastor Parish. He was trying hard not to show what he was feeling, because he was thinking that Sis Sally really needed to mind her own business and thank God that she was blessed enough not to be needy. "Does anyone else have any thoughts or concerns regarding the matter that Sis? Sally has brought to our attention?"

"I agree." This time it was Sis Be Be who spoke up. She stood to speak.

Deacon Douglass rolled his eyes to the back of his head wondering what his wife was about to complain about now.

"I agree with Sis. Sally, Pastor Parish. It seems like it's always the same people that the church is havin' to donate to all the time. Them same people don't never pay nothing, yet they steady got their hands out to get. I just don't think it's right that we keep on giving to them all the time. Judging by the clothes that some of em' wear whenever they do come up in here on Sundays, they ain't using it right no how."

First Lady Simone had been listening to the complaints as she sat quietly in her seat. She knew that both of the lady's complaints had been directed towards one specific person, and she was sure she knew just who that person was. She just didn't happen to share the same feelings about the matter. She could tell by the expression on her husband's face that he didn't agree either, but she knew that he didn't want to upset anybody. She weighed in her mind whether or not she should say something. Deciding that she should, she stood up to speak.

"Ladies, I'm not really clear on what it is that you see as a problem. Are you suggesting that you think some people are abusing the benevolent fund?" All eyes turned toward the First Lady. It wasn't often that she spoke out about most matters, but she was about to take on two of the oldest and most outspoken members of the board. So, she had everyone's full attention. Her husband eyed her nervously, not afraid for her, but more afraid for the two older women. His wife was most often the quiet observer type, but he knew that if and when she felt strongly enough about something the opposition had better watch out. Those ladies didn't know it, but they were about to be served a strong dose of The Word.

Simone continued. "Although I am not by any means the distributor of or the head over our benevolent department, I have worked closely with its leaders and I am not aware that anyone has ever come asking for a handout. Who we help is always decided upon by our very capable benevolent officers, and I am confident that they distribute the funds according to whomever they believe has a need. Colossians 3: 23-24 tells us that whatever we do, we should do it for the Lord and not men, and so that we might know that our reward shall come from the Lord whom we serve. Even if someone did come asking for help according to

Matthew 5: 42 we are to give to him that asketh thee, and not turn away from anyone needing to borrow. If we believe like we say we believe, then I think that we should be doing what the Word of God says and giving from our hearts. I don't think we should be worrying about who is getting what. We should leave that in the hands of the people who are in charge of that department. Our time would be better spent praising God for the blessings that he's going to give to us for our obedience to his will."

"Amen, Sister!" Responses of approval rang out across the sanctuary from several committee members who agreed.

Everyone knew that Simone was a woman of few words, but when she did have something to say, it was generally well received. Despite her age Simone was considered wise, even in the eyes of many of the older church mothers. She was like a quiet storm, not like those showy First Ladies that stood around in their fancy suits and hats looking all stiff and too cute to touch. Simone was, no doubt, a beautiful woman but also a very sweet, simple and kindhearted person. And, although it was usually her preference to avoid the spotlight, she did have a way of expressing herself in a very eloquent but matter-of-fact way when she was passionate about something.

Pastor Parish eyed his wife with secret pride as he watched her take her seat. When his gaze caught her eyes, he gave her a quick wink. Sis Sally James and Sis Be Be did not appear happy at all about what had been said, but Simone knew that they were rarely ever pleased with anything. Although she had a great respect for both women and their devotion to the church, Simone couldn't help but feel that they were critical of everything and always far too happy to have something to complain about.

"Are there any other comments or concerns regarding this particular issue that has been brought before us?" Pastor asked mostly as a formality rather than interest. As far as he was concerned, Simone had not only spoken what was in his heart, but she had also spoken the Word of God and there was just no substantial rebuttal for that. He was pleased when no one else spoke up, but not at all surprised. No one else he knew was more convincing than Simone when she had a point to prove. He'd learned that the hard way on several occasions over the years. They'd had many disagreements throughout their years of marriage, and he'd always been the one who had to surrender in the end. By the time she was done expressing her feelings and quoting scriptures to back up what she was saying, she just always left him with nothing else to argue. He saw his wife as wise, and he'd come to accept and appreciate that about her. Her wisdom had served as a constant source of inspiration in their lives, and in their ministry.

"I'll never take that woman for granted; I'm so blessed." he thought to himself.

They Don't Know Like I Know

Cleotis and Sally sat watching the 10:00 News just as they did every night before retiring to bed. Cleotis thought about the church meeting that they had attended earlier that evening.

"You know," he began, "First Lady Simone was right with what she said about that benevolent money. She sure is one sweet lady." Cleotis was very fond of the First Lady. Not only was she pretty, but she had her head on straight. In addition, she was one of the few people at Judah's Temple who treated him with respect. Other folks seemed to treat him like he was lower than they were because of his tendency to get drunk every now and then. Cleotis knew that some of those very same folk had a drink every now and then themselves on the down low. But Lady Simone never made him feel like he was less than, and he liked that about her.

His wife responded, "Yeah, she's sweet alright… naïve is what she really is." Not even his hyper-critical and overbearing wife could find anything that was really derogatory to say about Simone. "She's so naïve that she can't even see how that benevolent fund is just being bled dry by the few leeches that seem to be needing something all the time. They could just get a job like everybody else and stop laying around making all them illegitimate babies they can't take care of. But they all the time looking for a handout. Shucks, I got needs too, but you don't see me around asking nobody for nothing."

Cleotis sat and listened with fake interest at his wife's complaints. "If you did ask somebody for something, they probably wouldn't give it to you nohow, ugly as you're always acting toward folks," he thought to himself before he rose from his chair, mumbling a goodnight and heading off to bed.

Trouble in Paradise

Simone was putting away the last of the dinner dishes when her husband, who had just put the kids to bed, walked quietly up behind her and slipped his strong hands around her waist. He kissed her softly on her cheek and then on her neck, letting his lips glide further down until he'd reached her shoulders, where he gently placed another soft kiss. The warmth of his lips and breath on her neck made her tingle inside. A warm sensation spread through her body. She hunched her shoulders, indicating that he should stop and then turned to break the embrace that his arms had around her.

"Are the kids asleep?" she asked, moving towards the refrigerator to put away the leftovers. She knew that in his mind, he was questioning whether she had not accepted his affection. He was so sensitive. But she just wasn't in the mood for that yet; there was something on her mind and she knew that it was not going to be a welcomed topic.

"Yep, Jessica went to sleep as soon as her little head hit the pillow," her husband responded to her question. "But, you know who started pouting and trying to find reasons to avoid bedtime… same as usual. He's probably still in there pouting right about now."

"Well, that's our boy," Simone said jokingly as she giggled at the thought of Justin coming up with every imaginable excuse to try and avoid going to bed.

"No, that's your boy," her husband teased.

Simone dried her hands and then started toward the living room. Her husband followed, turning off the lights behind them as he did. Simone stopped briefly in the living room, bending to pick up the toys that the kids had left there. Playfully, her husband pinched her on the butt. She continued down the hallway. That wasn't the response that he'd hoped for. Simone stopped to peek in on the kids, her husband trailing quietly behind. She then headed toward their master bedroom, humming "His Eye Is on the Sparrow" as she went. The tune had been playing in her head all day long. She was thinking of how to go about approaching the matter that she was preparing to discuss with the pastor. It was a topic that usually brought tension between the two of them. Even though she felt like the matter had to be discussed, tension was not what she really wanted tonight. Although she hadn't let it be known, her husband's touches and kisses in the kitchen had aroused her. Now she wanted more. She looked over her shoulder, smiling at how he was following her so closely and looking at her with hungry eyes. What she really longed for most right now was to be held tightly in her husband's arms. However, there was something that needed to be discussed. She knew that if she didn't bring up what was bothering her right now, she might later think of it as irrelevant and place it in her memory until something else happens and causes the concern to resurface.

"Honey," she said softly as she sat on the lounge at the foot of the bed and reached out her hand to him, "can we talk about something?"

"Oh… oh, I can tell this is serious," Pastor Parish said, smiling sheepishly at his wife as he prepared himself to surrender yet again to whatever battle was brewing. He could tell by the serious look on her face that she was bothered about something.

"Have you talked with Julius about all the meetings he's missed lately?" Simone had barely gotten the word out of her mouth before she felt her husband's hands become tense. He quickly snatched them away and motioned with them abruptly in the air, obviously frustrated about the conversation that was about to take place.

"Ah, baby… here we go again!" was his loud and irritated reply.

Sensing his irritation, Simone quickly said, "Honey, I'm not trying to cause an argument, really. It's just that there are rules being broken and you don't seem concerned. Every time I try to ask about it, you get upset. You're always saying that in the house of the Lord, things should be done decently and in order. And it's like you expect everybody to abide by the rules of the house… except Julius. I'm sorry, but that just doesn't seem fair to me. You can't just keep ignoring what he does."

Julius Magee, known around Judah's Temple as the Honorable Rev. Magee, was one of Pastor Parish's oldest friends. Simone had met them both in college. The two had roomed together until she and Pastor got married in their senior year. Julius had earned the reputation of being a lady's man on campus. Simone had suspected that most of what she heard about him was probably true. There were always different girls in and out of the guy's apartment all the time. Pastor seemed to not think much of it back then; he'd say, "That's just Julius's way, it's none of my business."

"Now, Simone, you know that I treat all of my ministers with respect. I've never had one complaint."

"You do treat them with respect, honey, but are you being fair in your expectations for all of them? Just because they haven't complained to you yet doesn't mean that they haven't noticed."

"Simone, you're making a big deal out of nothing. Why do you hate him so much? I thought you'd have gotten over all that college stuff by now. He's a preacher now for God's sake, why can't you just let it all go?!"

Simone replied, "This is not about anything that has to do with college; it's about the business of the church. Why do you always have to get so defensive when I mention his name? I'm just trying to say that even though no one's complained yet, you can be sure that people have noticed. Someone will complain one day. What will you do then?"

"You know what, Simone, I don't think that this is even worth talking about right now. There isn't a problem and no one's going to complain because there is nothing to complain about. I treat all of my people in leadership positions the same. Where I might make allowances for Julius in one way, I make allowances for somebody else in another way. Now, I don't care to talk about this any further. So, I'm done with this conversation!" Pastor Parish headed out of the bedroom, closing the door behind him.

Simone was furious. "Why does he always have to be so defensive when we talk about Julius?" she thought as she walked into the adjoining bathroom to shower and slammed the door behind her. Was he too blind to see that this thing was going to cause him trouble if he didn't deal with it soon? Heck, it had already caused trouble because tonight, instead of hugging each other, they would be hugging opposite corners of their king-sized bed.

Wednesday Night Service

"That sure was one heartfelt sermon you preached this evening, Pastor," one of the members said, shaking the pastor's hand on his way out. It was the custom of their church for the pastor and his wife to stand at the church doors and greet everyone on their way out. No one would have guessed that the two of them were feeling anything less than complete adoration for each other, even now. They'd learned never to let their personal feelings and affairs at home interfere with the business at church. But deep down inside, Simone was still fuming from the argument that they'd had a few nights before.

When the last person had exited the sanctuary, without a word to her husband, Simone turned and started toward the pastor's study. The look that she had seen in her husband's eyes before turning away let her know that he was hopeful she was not still upset. But she'd rolled her eyes at him purposefully to indicate that she was. She wasn't going to pretend that everything was okay. He wouldn't get off quite that easily.

Simone was about to turn the corner to enter the large pastoral quarters, which contained a conference room and five small but sufficient offices belonging to the pastor and four associate ministers. But she stopped briefly when she heard what sounded like moaning coming from behind the doors of one of the rooms. As she walked on, the sounds became more distinguishable. They were moans, and they were coming from Julius's office. She couldn't help but wonder what was going on behind those closed doors. She had her suspicions, but she sure couldn't tell her husband about them. She shook her head and continued to walk across the hall and into her husband's office. She kept her eyes locked on Julius's door as she slipped into her trench coat and grabbed her kids' jackets. The moaning grew louder and then stopped. She thought she heard whispering and a lot of shuffling around. She was sure that she'd also heard someone giggle. Simone loudly shuffled some papers around on her husband's desk to make her presence known.

"Praise the Lord," she recognized Julius's voice. His office door opened, and out came a young woman whose face Simone recognized as someone she had seen before out in the congregation. As she got a better look, Simone realized that the young woman was actually one of the church's newest members. She had just recently joined the church a few Sundays ago. Simone recognized her from one of the new members' meetings that she and Pastor Parish had attended to introduce themselves.

As the young woman exited the office door, she dabbed at her eyes with a small hankie. "Thank you for your help," she exclaimed with a soft whine and whimper, no doubt aware of the fact that Simone was watching. "Anytime, my sister, and God bless you," was Rev. Magee's slick reply. He stood in the doorway to watch her leave. As he turned to go back into his office, his eyes met Simone's. She quickly glanced away and pretended to be busy organizing something in the office. She knew exactly what she had just witnessed, but how would she ever be able to convince her husband that it had happened when he was always so eager to defend Julius?

Rev. Magee was aware that Simone had been watching. He wondered if she suspected anything. He thought about making an effort to explain to her that he had just ministered to the poor lost soul, but he decided against it. "Even if she does suspect something, what's she gonna do?" he reasoned with himself. He wasn't too worried about her running to her husband. After all, he was the reason why her husband held the title 'Pastor' at this church. He'd used his family influence to help his friend get the position. And besides that, he knew something about her husband that she didn't. He also knew that her husband would do almost anything to keep it that way because if she ever found out, she would be devastated. His devoted friend would never risk that because he loved her too much. "I've got no reason to worry. That's my dog... my partner... we go way back. He'd never turn on me," he thought out loud as he grabbed his jacket and prepared to lock up and head home for the evening.

Simone waited until he'd left before she exited to go pick up the kids from the children's church. She got an eerie feeling thinking about the coldness that she had just seen in Julius's face when their eyes had briefly met during the encounter. His stare was almost daring. This was not the first time that she had questioned situations involving Julius and various female members of the church. She felt in her spirit that there was merit to her concerns. She knew she couldn't prove anything, and she didn't know where she would even begin. Nevertheless, she decided that something was going to have to be done.

Simone hadn't noticed Cleotis sweeping the hallway earlier when she had come in. "Hi, Mr. Cleotis," she nodded, her mind still occupied by the things that had just taken place. "Afternoon, First Lady," Cleotis responded, avoiding eye contact. He wondered if she had just witnessed the same thing that he had.

God Knows

Sis Be Be turned the chicken that she had frying on the stove. They'd had fried chicken for dinner every Sunday for as long as she could remember. Sis Be Be had grown tired of it and wanted to have something different occasionally, but her husband insisted on the continuation of the tradition. "Damn, I forgot to find out what time the youth choir was returning from their trip," she spoke out loud as she lifted the lid on the pot of turnip greens. She didn't know it, but her husband, Deacon Douglass had slipped up behind her, "a Christian woman ain't supposed to be cussing like that. What would the Pastor think?" He chuckled. "Go to hell," was her response, "The Pastor aint got to know everything that goes on everywhere." Her husband let out a loud hearty laugh. "You right about that, Baby!" He was feeling frisky, he placed his hand on his wife's thigh, "he sho' wouldn't need to know about what you did to me last night… now would he," he whispered in her ear. He knew this would both catch her off guard and get her attention because for years now, they had routinely had sex together only once a month, usually more out of obligation than anything else. It was all that his wife would allow. However, since he had started taking Viagra, he wanted so much more. But Be Be wasn't having it. Once a month was all that she was willing to give. That's why he had sought the companionship of sweet ole Betty Jean. Betty Jean was a much younger woman who worked at his law firm office. Betty Jean said she couldn't meet him today when he had called her earlier… Something about her ex-husband. So, Deacon thought to himself, "I guess Be

Be's gone have to do." Deacon Douglas enjoyed the intimate company of his wife some, but she had too many hang-ups about what was and was not ok for the bedroom. Betty Jean, on the other hand, gave him whatever he wanted, just the way he wanted, and as much as he wanted. He preferred the way that Betty Jean took care of his needs, but Betty Jean wasn't here, and he needed some attention right now. He had come home from church today thinking about all those fine young women that he'd seen in their short, tight fitting, low-cut dresses. "It was getting to the point where it's hard to concentrate on the Lord," he'd thought to himself earlier today while taking up the collection, "with all those thighs, butts and breasts just hanging out everywhere....and right there in your face." Still aroused from Sunday services, Deacon Douglass had come in from church and gone straight to his office where he kept his stash of girlie pictures and X-rated videos. Not even his nosey wife knew about his collection. This was his private business; he couldn't risk her knowing and take the chance of having someone else find out about his little secret one day if she happened to throw one of her little fits of rage like she so often did when she wasn't getting her way. He could not take a chance on her telling anybody. This was for his eyes and ears only. If anyone ever found out about something like this, he could lose his standing in the church and in the community. Heck, he might even be kicked out of his position as head deacon, and he was not willing to risk that. He was convinced that people would think hard of him if they knew, but his philosophy was 'what they don't know won't hurt them'. Besides, he reasoned, if Be Be was doing her job as his wife he wouldn't have to resort to such measures. He felt justified in his need for his little stash. After all, if he couldn't get what he wanted from his wife, then he should at least be able to get some satisfaction from watching it. He wasn't hurting anybody, and it was no one else's business.

"What's gotten into you?" Sis Be Be turned to look at him. "Man, now I just slept with you last night. After hearing that good sermon today at church, I ain't trying to defile myself. I'm trying to keep my mind stayed on Jesus. I ain't got time for you and your lustful foolishness today."

"What do you mean you ain't got time for my lustful foolishness? You're my wife, woman. There ain't nothing lustful about a man and his wife having relations. And you weren't worried about keeping your mind stayed on Jesus a few minutes ago when you was doing all that cussin'," Deacon said and turned away, annoyed.

"You go to hell," she spat as her husband left the kitchen, heading back down the hall to his office. She heard him slam the door and then lock it. The doorbell rang.

"Who in the hell is this?" she said, throwing the dish towel onto the counter and going to answer the door. In a most delightful voice, she said, "Oh Cleotis, it's so good to see you. Come on in. I'm not going to ask how you're doing today, 'cause I know you're being blessed."

Cleotis had heard yelling before he reached to ring the doorbell. He'd thought about coming back by later but decided that it was just going to be too inconvenient. He played along.

"The Lord's keepin' me," he said. "I couldn't complain if I wanted to."

"I know that's right. He's good like that, ain't he?" Be Be replied. "You looking for the Deacon? He's down the hall there in that office of his. Just go on down the hall there and knock on the door." She faked the sweetest smile as she pointed the way.

Deacon Douglass had forgotten that he'd told Cleotis to stop by this afternoon to pick up his check. Deacon Douglass was in charge of the church funds, and in his rush to make it to church on time, he'd forgotten the paychecks that morning. Cleotis had been a custodian at the church for years.

Deacon Douglass had just put one of his girlie flicks into the VCR. He had not expected his wife or daughter to come anywhere near his office, which was off to one corner of the house all by itself, so he had made no effort to secure his door. He was caught off guard when he looked up to see Cleotis entering. He made a dash for the power button on the VCR and pushed it as quickly as he could. He wasn't sure whether Cleotis had seen anything or not. He tried to read the expression on his face as he turned to greet him with a firm handshake.

"Bro. Cleotis, how's it going, man?" he said loudly, chuckling and trying hard not to look as guilty as he felt. "I sho' hope he didn't see anything," he thought to himself. Little did he know that Cleotis had seen plenty enough to know that he had surely not been watching the Christian channel. But he could feel the Deacon's discomfort and saw no reason to make him squirm anymore, so he decided to get right to the point.

"You told me to stop by and pick up my pay."

"Oh, yeah man, I sure did. Ok, let me get that for you. This sure is good weather we havin' lately, ain't it?" Deacon moved toward the safe where he kept the money in his office.

"Um hum, it has been mighty nice lately." Cleotis joined him in the small talk.

"You gone catch any of the game today?" Deacon asked. "I was just trying to get my TV here all set up and ready for it. I can't hardly enjoy no game in the family room without the women folk botherin' me. So, I watch in here mostly." He fidgeted nervously with the lock on the safe before getting it open. "I expect, though, that when I get me a belly full of somethin' to eat, the TV is going to be watching me." He slapped his knee as he let out a hearty laugh.

Cleotis chuckled too. "I hear you. I expect I'll do the same unless the boss lady has somethin' else for me to do when I get home… you know how that goes." He chuckled some more. "I got to go in to work for a little while tonight, though, so I won't get to see the whole game."

The Deacon interjected, "I know what you mean, man. There's always something to do."

"You sho' right about that," Cleotis responded. An awkward moment of silence followed his reply. "Well, I better be headin' home now, Deacon, before the old lady sends out a search party."

"Alright, man. I'll see you later. You be blessed now, OK."

"Same to you," Cleotis responded, heading back up the hall toward the door. "You have a good evening, Mrs. Smith," he said as he passed by the kitchen. She nodded. Cleotis saw himself out the door. "That sure was an awkward encounter," he thought to himself on his way down the front door steps.

What's done in the Dark

Kiara sat out in the car, waiting for Bro. Rossi to check them in and return with the room key. "This hotel is whack," she mumbled out loud. "He never takes me anywhere nice anymore."

She'd wanted this to be a special night. She'd gone through the trouble of making a trip to the other side of town just to sneak into a lingerie shop to buy a sexy outfit and some candles. It was exactly four months ago that they'd first made love. She'd convinced her best friend, Kelly, to make the trip across town on the bus with her. They'd spent the whole day planning how to make the occasion as grown-up and romantic as possible. They shared ideas that they'd seen in the movies and magazines. Kiara had also managed to purchase a bottle of wine from a kid at school. She'd wanted this to be a night to remember, but she was beginning to wonder why she'd even bothered. He'd said that they would go somewhere nice. But this place sure didn't look like what she'd imagined. "Oh well, we'll just make the best of it," she told herself. "All that really matters is that we're together."

Bro. Rossi came out of the motel lobby, clenching the key in one hand and smiling from ear to ear. He opened the car door and slid into the seat. "Did you miss me, muffin?" he said, leaning over to kiss Kiara on the neck.

"I don't care where I am as long as I'm with him," she thought. She felt as though her body was melting in her seat. The couple pulled around until they had reached the point where they could see their motel room number on the door. They got out and went to the door. Just as Bro. Rossi had slipped the key into the door and opened it slightly, something quickly scurried across the floor.

Kiara screamed like someone was losing their mind. "I can't do this! Take me home, NOW!"

Cleotis wondered what all the screaming was about. He put his mop in the bucket and turned to glance in the direction from which the noise had come. He was shocked at what he saw.

"That's Deacon Douglass's little girl and that no-good piano player from church," he mumbled to himself. He could not believe his eyes. He'd heard rumors about the musician being a womanizer and all, but he never would have thought he'd be messing around with young girls. Cleotis ducked into a corner to make sure they didn't see him. What on earth would the Smiths do if they knew about this? As much as he and Sally had sometimes been so saddened by never having had children, he was certainly glad that he didn't have a daughter right about now. He watched as the two got into the car and sped off into the night. He shook his head and then returned to his work. He wanted to hurry and get finished. After seeing what he'd just seen, he was going to need to stop off for a drink or two before going home.

Family First

Pastor Parish wondered what was taking Simone so long to come out of the house. He had already loaded the cooler, drinks, and kids into the car. He tooted the horn.

"Simone, honey, come on. We're going to be late."

They had planned a family outing today. First, they'd catch a movie, then they'd have a picnic in the park and go for a walk. On the way back home, they'd stop for some ice cream. Pastor thought that this was exactly what the family needed. Simone loved family time, and she had been a little edgy lately. He thought some time with the family would be good for her. He longed to see that smile on her face that made each day so bright. She hadn't been too happy with him lately, and he knew why, but he wanted to get past that now. He missed the intimacy that he and his wife usually shared.

"Simone," he yelled again.

Simone emerged from the front door with an irritated look on her face. "I'm coming!" She hoped that her response hadn't been as snappy as it had sounded. She knew that lately, she had probably come across as being a little irritated with her husband. But she couldn't help it. She had to figure out a way to get him to see that ignoring the actions of his best friend in the church was not the Godly thing to do.

"Lord, you're going to have to help me with this one. I don't know what to do, but I refuse to let this come between me and my husband," she prayed on her way down the steps.

"I'm coming," she said again, this time in a much softer and controlled tone. "I'm sorry, I just wanted to make sure that the baby bag was restocked with all the things we need."

With that, she hopped in on the passenger side of the car, closed the door, and off they went.

Only God Can Judge Me

"Cleotis!" Sally yells at the top of her voice with a sense of urgency. "Come in here, now!"

"What is it now, woman?" Cleotis yelled back.

"Sister Lola just called and told me that she saw you last night coming out of that liquor store. She said you staggered all the way to the car. She said that she started to call and let me know last night, but that she didn't want to upset me before I went to bed. Now, Cleotis… I've told you about going around this town embarrassing me like that. You're just an old drunken fool!" Sally continued to yell.

"Now you listen, Sally…" Cleotis makes an attempt to defend himself.

"Listen to you??? Now, why in the hell would I listen to you?" Sally spat back. "What can you tell me??? You're so weak and stupid that you don't even have enough sense to stay sober. The least you could do when you go and get drunk is to stay in the damn house so that nobody sees you. You know how people around here talk. I get sick and tired of people around here looking at me sideways and snickering because of your drunk ass. I'm a prominent church worker. I have a reputation to uphold." Sally crosses her arms and frowns at Cleotis with a disgusted look on her face.

Cleotis responded, "You sure worry enough about what I do and what other people think. I wonder what other people would think if they saw how you were talking to me right now. I might not know much, but I don't think anything in that Bible that you claim to read so often says it's OK for you to talk to and treat me the way that you do sometimes."

Cleotis could usually hold his temper and ignore his wife's ranting and raving pretty well, but he just didn't feel like hearing it today. Knowing some of what he knew about some of those nosy so-called 'Saints' who always felt a need to call and report what he was doing, he had become quite fed up with folks watching and criticizing his every move. It was true that he had a drink or two… or maybe even five every now and then, but that was between him and God. Other people had no right to judge him and be so self-righteous.

Cleotis started again, "You're always worrying about what somebody thinks about you. My sins are my own, and anyway… you should be worrying more about what God thinks about you. You walk around here trying to look like the world's most saved Christian… you and the rest of your holy roller friends."

As Cleotis turns to leave, he grabs his jacket from the closet and heads toward the front door. He was tired of being judged and treated like the town idiot because he liked to drink. "Who do they think they are anyways," he mumbled to himself, "They ain't no better than I am." He slams the door on the way out. He needed a drink!

Missing In Action

AMAZING GRACE

HOW SWEET THE SOUND

THAT SAVED A WRETCH

LIKE ME......

Where was he? Amazing grace was already being sung, and Julius had still not shown up. He was scheduled to deliver the sermon today. Pastor Parish begins to worry about his friend. He is also getting a little anxious about the possibility of having to deliver a sermon that he has not prepared for. Since it wasn't his regular Sunday to preach, he had spent all of his free time with his family this week instead of preparing for a sermon. He had a few sermons that he could possibly pull out of his hat, but he was never comfortable with delivering the word of God without prayer and preparation. He'd always believed that it just didn't do God's word justice to deliver it any old kind of way. Pastor Parish begins to feel agitated. It seemed as though he was losing a handle on so many things lately. Several of the organizations within the church were having problems and disagreements, one right after the other, and then there were his problems with Simone. She just wasn't herself lately. He couldn't put his finger on exactly what it was, but he couldn't help but feel as though something had changed. Simone had been very quiet and reserved lately and a little too agreeable. It was almost like she was carefully filtering what she said and how she responded to him. Up until lately, he and Simone had been very open with each other, and she had never been one to bite her tongue. On top of all his other problems right now, were all the problems that Julius was causing lately by not pulling his weight in the ministry. Other ministers had begun to complain about how he has been showing up late for appointments or not at all. They'd also been complaining about the fact that several duties that had been assigned to him were not being carried out in the proper way. Pastor Parish just couldn't understand what had gotten into his friend lately. Julius could get a little out of hand sometimes, but he usually always came through. They had always had each other's backs.

As the congregation begins to hum Amazing Grace, Pastor Parish rises to his feet and walks over to stand behind the podium. He begins to hum into the microphone. Simone notices that her husband looks a little tense standing there in the pulpit. She knew that he had not planned on delivering the sermon that day. The song ends, and just as Pastor Parish instructs the congregation to be seated, he notices Julius entering the pulpit out of the corner of his eye. "It's going to be hard, but I'm going to have to have a talk with him very soon," he thinks to himself as he acknowledges Julius and turns the pulpit over to his long-time dear friend.

After church, Pastor Parish sits in his office, looking over committee reports and thinking about what he was going to say to Julius. He had intended to have a talk with his good friend after church, but Julius had rushed out immediately after dismissal saying that he had to attend an important family engagement. Julius's parents were very influential in the community and were often required to attend big affairs. Julius was single and still lived at home with his parents, so he often tagged along with them from one event to another, more for the attention that he got than for any other reason.

Pastor Parish is deep in thought and does not notice Simone when she enters his office.

"Honey," She says to get his attention.

"Yes Simone."

"This isn't worth it."

"What are you talking about?" Pastor Parish tries to keep a calm and straight face like nothing is wrong as he turns in his chair to face his wife.

"Protecting Julius and letting him worry you like this. It's not good."

"Ah, Simone…. I don't want to go through this with you right now."

Pastor Parish grew agitated at what his wife was saying. He knew that he was going to have to talk to Julius soon. But he couldn't help but feel that Simone had never cared much for his friendship with Julius, which had always been a source of torment for him. He loved his wife more than anything, but Julius had always been a loyal friend to him… especially during a major crisis that he had endured during the first year after he and Simone had married. They'd had a very trying first year of marriage, several times threatening to end it in divorce. Simone had never been made aware of a personal crisis that he had encountered during that time….and which most likely would have ended their marriage for sure. Pastor Parish and Julius had both agreed that she never needed to know, and they had made a pact to keep it between the two of them. Julius had been a constant source of support for him during those tough times, and Pastor Parish could not simply forget how loyal he had been.

"I know you don't want to hear it, but you are ignoring all these things that Julius is doing wrong instead of dealing with them, it's affecting others, and it's affecting you too whether you'll admit to it or not!" She hadn't meant for it to, but Simone's voice had escalated in anger as she tried to make her point.

"Simone, I don't need you to tell me how to do my job!" Pastor Parish's voice rose in response. "I didn't ask for your opinion, and it's not your place! I'm the pastor of this church. I'll let you know when I need your help pastoring my church! Right now, all I need your help with is getting the kids so that we can all go home!"

Simone was furious. How dare he talk to her that way! She couldn't remember a time when she had ever felt the kinds of emotions she was feeling right now. It took all the effort she had to keep from cussing her husband out right there where he stood, in his Pastor's study. "Who does he think he is… talking to me like that???" Simone's thoughts raced back and forth in her head. She turned to leave but then quickly decided that she needed to let her husband know just what was on her mind. Before she could get the words out, the Holy Spirit quickens her and James 1:26 comes to mind…..

If anyone considers himself religious and yet does not keep a tight rein on his tongue, he deceives himself and his religion is worthless.

Simone decided that it was best for her to hold her tongue….at least for now. She said a silent prayer asking God to help her to be obedient to his word and then turned to head for the Children's church to pick up the kids. As she exits the office and rounds the corner, she bumps into Cleotis, who is sweeping the floor. He stops sweeping and pushes the vacuum cleaner to the side out of her way.

"I'm sorry, Mr. Cleotis, I should watch where I'm going," Simone said apologetically, avoiding eye contact.

"Aw, ain't no harm done, First Lady……" Cleotis noticed the tears falling down Simone's face. "Are you alright? Is there something that I can do for ya?" Cleotis asked with sincere concern.

"No sir, Mr. Cleotis. I'll be fine." She said, faking a smile. "But thank you for asking." Simone continued down the hall. She stopped by the lady's room to wipe her tear-stained face. She wondered if Mr. Cleotis had heard the fighting between her and her husband. Cleotis watched her as she exited the ladies' room and continued walking down the hall toward the Children's church. He had been sweeping the room next door, and although he wished he hadn't, he had heard the whole argument. "Poor thing," he thought sadly to himself while shaking his head.

The wages of Sin

Kiarra sits in the bay window of her best friend's bedroom with her head buried in her hands and tears streaming down her face. "What am I going to do? My parents are going to kill me!" Kiarra is sobbing profusely. Kelly gently rubs her friend's back and tries to soothe her. "I don't know how this could have happened.....he says that he pulls out in time when we do it."

"Are you telling me that you guys have been having sex without a condom?" Kelly says with a surprised look on her face. "What were you thinking Kiarra? I knew this would all come to no good. The Bible says that fornication is wrong…"

"I know, I know… Kelly. We should have used something, but he said he didn't like the way it felt with condoms, and I couldn't get birth control without my parents finding out. They would kill me if they knew I was having sex."

"Well, how are you gonna hide it from them now? Kiarra, I tried to tell you that what you were doing was wrong, but you wouldn't listen. What are you gonna do now?" Kelly is both concerned and scared for Kiarra. She begins to pray and asks God to help her to know how to help her friend.

"Oh God!" Kiarra cries out. "I don't know what I'm going to do, please help me." Her sobs grow harder and louder.

Kelly was glad that her parents were not home. They had gone out to dinner leaving the two teenagers there alone for a few hours. She wraps her arms around her friend and tries to console her. Together,they rock back and forth in silence for what seems like hours. Kelly breaks the silence with her words of encouragement. "Kiarra, I'm your friend, and I'm here for you. But I don't know what to do. We're going to have to find someone who can help."

"No! We can't tell anybody." Kiarra said breathlessly between sobs. "I don't want anyone to know. My parents cannot find out that I'm pregnant!" She yells and starts to tremble frantically.

"OK, OK. You have to calm down, Kiarra. You're going to make yourself sick….and we have to get you some help. Give me some time to think about this. Everything will be alright. You'll see. This is going to work out somehow. God will see us through."

Kelly wasn't sure that she even believed her own words at this point, but she had to do what she could to help her friend. She begins to pray again. "Dear Lord, you said that you would never leave us or forsake us. My friend has done wrong Lord, but she needs you right now. Please Lord, help my friend."

What to Do

Cleotis sits at the bar thinking about some of the things that he'd witnessed lately. Cleotis had never been one to get into other folks' business. Lord knows he sure wished others would stay out of his. But he couldn't stop thinking about seeing Deacon Douglass's little girl at that motel with that slimy musician. He had also been thinking a lot about the argument that he accidentally overheard between the Pastor and First Lady. He knew that the First Lady had been right. Rev. Magee had women going in and out of his office for one reason or another all the time, and the noises that came out of his office while he was in there with those women didn't usually sound like holy ones. "Lord, this world is getting to be a mess," he mumbles to himself as he signals the bartender for another beer. "Saints sure can be funny." He thinks to himself. "They look like new money on Sunday all dressed up in their suits, hats and fine shoes. But underneath all them pretty clothes, some of them are just as messed up as everybody else….Then, they got the nerve to look down on folks like me as if they think they more saved than I am because of my drinking. But the truth is, they're not. They what you call Sunday Saints…. cause they full of hell the rest of the days of the week. Well, to hell with all of them, 'cause that's where they are all going anyway."

Cleotis lays money on the bar to cover his tab, and motions to the bartender that he is leaving. Just as he swirls around on the bar stool and stands to leave, he catches a glimpse of a familiar face. He had purposely chosen this bar because of its location. It was far enough from home that he wouldn't have expected to run into anyone he knew. So, he was quite surprised to see Deacon Douglass having dinner at a table in a dark corner of the pub. He was even more surprised that Deacon Douglass appeared to be feeding shrimp to an attractive young woman who looked half his age. It was obvious to Cleotis that Deacon Douglass had probably also chosen this location so that he wouldn't have to worry about running into anyone he knew. Cleotis decided that it was probably best for him to make a quick exit before he was spotted. He certainly didn't want to chance word of his drinking getting back to his wife. He was in no mood to hear her mouth tonight. Cleotis ordered a bottle of liquor to go and headed toward the door. Having had far too much to drink already, he staggered to his car, hopped in and then sped off. Deacon Douglass looked up from his dessert menu and peered out the window to notice what he thought was a familiar looking man in a familiar looking car spinning out quickly.

"Was that??"...He wasn't aware that he was speaking aloud.

"What?" His date looked around for what had all of a sudden captured his attention.

"Oh, nothing, darling. I just thought for a minute that I saw someone I know. Nothing for you to worry your pretty head about."

BettyJean grinned at the Deacon, her new gold tooth that the deacon had just purchased for her shining through her smile.

"You decided what you wanna eat for dessert yet, my little Philly?" Deacon asks. "It's been so long that I can't wait to get you to that hotel and get my hands on you. Big daddy got something good in store for you tonight." Deacon was so anxious that he was practically salivating as he spoke.

"I got something good for you too big daddy," She giggled as she slipped off her pumps and reached with her feet underneath the table to gently stroke the rise that she knew she would find in his pants. Betty stroked away, thinking about what she was going to buy with the shopping money that he was sure to give her tonight.

"Order me some more of them Scrimps, Big Daddy." She said, giving him a seductive grin.

"Anything you want, baby…anything you say."

The Wolf in Sheep's Clothing

Rev. Magee adjusted his shirt collar and glanced at his reflection in the window. "Looking good." He thought to himself as he reached to ring the doorbell again. He wondered what's taking Ciara so long to answer the door, she had known that he would be dropping by that evening. It hadn't been easy, but he had been working hard to wear her down and help her to forget about all those inhibitions that she had about having sex without being married. The fact that he was a preacher had made it even more of a challenge. But he was certain that he'd win, and he planned to be collecting on his winnings any day now. "Come on baby, hurry up and answer the door." He mumbled, turning toward the street and looking around nervously to make sure that no one was watching. He couldn't be too careful. He didn't want any of those noisy church folks to see him and start spreading rumors. The folks at church were already acting kind of funny toward him lately. Complaining about one thing that he hadn't done or another. Of course he would never have said it to anyone, but his personal feeling was that they all just needed to mind their own business. He wasn't hurting anybody. Sure, he loved the women, but he wasn't forcing any of them to do anything that they didn't want to do. The way he saw it, he wasn't doing any more wrong than anybody else, and God would forgive him for his sins too.

The door finally opened. In front of him stood Ciara with red, swollen eyes and looking very disheveled. She was wearing a big, bulky robe, and her hair was all over her head.

"She's tore up from the floor up." Is the first thought that ran through his mind. Ciara had called the church earlier to speak with someone in the single's ministry. Rev. Magee had been the one to answer the phone. She was very distraught as she told him about her baby's daddy just up and deciding that he wanted to be with someone else. "Baby Mama Drama," Rev. Magee had thought to himself when he had taken the call. It was typical for one of the women ministers to have handled such a case, but when he'd realized who it was that was calling, he'd decided to handle this case himself. He'd had his eyes on this one for quite some time. He'd seen her come to church with her son often, but she'd also brought a man along once or twice too. Rev. Magee knew this because once when he was admiring her during the church service, when he accidentally made eye contact with her gentleman friend. The icy gaze that he had received as the guy stared back in his direction had been none too friendly.

Ciara led Rev. Magee to the living room sofa and offered him a seat. She grabbed some tissues from the coffee table and began speaking.

"I just don't know what I'm gonna do." She sobbed.

"I know this is hard, but I'm here for you sister." Rev. Magee pretended to be interested in her problem. But what he is really interested in is the bit of cleavage that he notices firmly protruding from behind her robe. He licks his lips and makes an effort to try and listen as Ciara continues on with her story. Ciara paused to dab away at the tears that were streaming down her face.

59

"Now that he's made it to the pros, he's left me for somebody else. I'm the one who had his son, and who has stuck by his side all throughout college. I've had to work to support all three of us for the last 3 years, and now he's leaving me." Her sobs grew more intense.

Rev. Magee attempted to console her. "I know it hurts, but it's gonna be Ok." He says taking her in his arms and rubbing her back gently. But as he does so, his mind wonders. He can't help but to think how good she feels in his arms. Realizing that he's becoming turned on, he releases her. He doesn't want to risk pushing her away by reacting too eagerly, too soon. He stared into her eyes, then gently caressed her cheek with the back of his hand. "A real man would never have hurt such a beautiful woman like that. I couldn't imagine ever treating someone like you that way. I've been watching you for a while now, thinking what a blessing it would be to have a woman like you. I can tell that you're a special kind of lady... and you deserve a special kind of man. One that will love and take care of you. If I had someone so beautiful, I would never hurt you." He pulled her close to him. He is satisfied with the eager response that she gives him as he places his hand on her thigh and begins to caress it ever so gently. He then lands a soft lingering kiss on her willing lips.

"Rev. Magee?"

"Hum." He responds with a soft, sultry whisper in her ear.

"I know this isn't right. We're not married, and you're a preacher, but I just need to feel loved right now."

"I understand, my dear. Let me give you what you need. I'll bet I can make you feel better."

Rev. Magee stands and takes Ciarra by the hand, staring deep into her eyes as he kisses her passionately. Ciarra, feeling torn and confused but needy, guides him toward her bedroom. She is glad that her son's father had decided to keep him for a few days after he had stopped by to inform her that they would no longer be together.

"Bingo!" Rev. Magee thinks to himself, trying hard to hide his enthusiasm so that he doesn't appear too eager. "I've scored again!"

Touching and Agreeing

Simone has just laid down, purposely turning her back toward her husband, when she felt his strong arms wrap around her. She knew that her husband needed her. It's been almost a whole week since they'd been intimate, and she needed him too. But she hadn't been able to forget the unresolved fight that they'd had, and her body grew tense at his touch. He sensed the tension, drew his arms back and then propped himself up on his elbows facing the direction of his wife. He beckoned for her to turn to face him….and with some reluctance, she did.

"Simone," He began. "How long is this going to go on?"

"I don't know what you're talking about," Simone responded nonchalantly.

"Yes, you do. You've been acting like this ever since our discussion about Julius."

Staring directly into her husband's eyes, Simone declared, "Correction, we didn't have a discussion. A discussion is when two people both talk and both listen. I would not call what we did a discussion".

"Honey," Pastor Parish looked at his wife…his eyes pleading, "I don't think that we should really be arguing about this. This is ridiculous."

"What's ridiculous," Simone insisted, "is how you refuse to see the truth."

"Simone…. look baby…I'm sorry. I don't want to argue about this anymore. I need you right now, Pastor Parish exclaimed as he reached out for his wife.

Simone was still angry with her husband, but she had never been one to let her emotions keep her from being a wife. She surrendered herself to her husband freely, relishing his every touch and enjoying the way that he made her feel.

When Trouble Comes

"I came home as soon as I could. What's the big emergency?" Deacon Douglass had rushed out of his office when his wife called crying hysterically and begging him to come home.

"You need to sit down." Sis Be Be said, looking very serious through tear-streaked eyes. She had regained her composure by now, but her eyes were still puffy, and Deacon Douglass could tell that something was really wrong.

"It's Kiarra."

Deacon Douglass interrupted. "Kiarra??!! Where is she? She's not hurt, is she? Is she OK?" He is talking so fast that his words are running together.

"Calm down now, calm down. It's nothing like that." Sis Be Be reassured.

'What is it then?" Deacon Douglass nervously questioned. It was obvious that he was getting anxious.

Sis Be Be pondered how to begin. "Kiarra is," she pauses for a moment, "she is pregnant." Each word felt like a sharp needle piercing her tongue as she said it. She still could not believe that her precious little girl had gone and gotten herself pregnant. "How could this have happened, and what are people going to think?"

Deacon sat in silence for a while. The expression on his face showed a mixture of confusion and shock. He gathers himself and is finally able to speak.

"Pregnant………pregnant, how could this be? That's my little baby."

"Yeah, well apparently she's not your little baby anymore." Sis Be Be retorted.

Still not totally sure how to feel, Deacon Douglass suddenly becomes irate. "Who did this to her!! Who is he? I'll kill him!!"

"Man, you can't just go around killing people. She was there when it happened too, you know. Are you gonna kill her too??? Besides, she won't say who's it is. Quite frankly, I can't see how that all matters much at this point anyway." Said Be Be in an unusually calm and somber voice which was not typical for her…especially given the circumstances.

Deacon Douglass buried his face in the palms of his hands and began to sob. He felt powerless, and in this moment did not know what else to do.

"Ain't much use in crying about it? That won't solve nothing. I've already made the appointment for her to get an abortion tomorrow," Said Be Be. "We'll be leaving early in the morning since it's a three-hour drive to the clinic. I'm taking her to one far away so that nobody finds out about this. I already spoke with the nurse at her school. She's the one who called to let me know about this. She promises that this information will be kept confidential. God forbid that nosey Sis Sally James find out about this. She'll have it spread across town before you can blink your eyes. I don't want everybody looking at me sideways because of this mess."

Deacon Douglass glared at his wife. He couldn't believe her attitude about this ordeal. She only seemed to be concerned about herself. In an angry tone he shouted, "Is that all you can think about….people looking at you funny??? Our little girl is pregnant, and you're worried about yourself. I knew you were selfish, Be Be, but I never thought you'd care more about how you look than your own daughter!"

Sis Be Be yelled back. "What can I do about the fact that she's pregnant? Not a damn thing! If it hadn't been for you always putting your precious little girl on a pedestal and letting her think that she could have and do whatever she wanted, then maybe she wouldn't be in this mess anyway!"

Deacon Douglass got up from where he was seated and began to walk away. "Go ahead, Be Be, blame it on me just like you always do. Everything is all my fault, as usual. It always is. I'm leaving. I'll be back later."

"Where are you going?" Be Be yells, trailing behind him as he heads for the door. "Run like you always do. You coward! All you have ever been good for is your money, anyway. Go ahead, leave!"

Deacon Douglass leaves, slamming the door loudly behind him.

Kiarra had been in her room trying to sleep. Today had been a hard day, and lately she had been crying so much that she was exhausted. The slamming of the door had awakened her. She got up to look out her bedroom window. She saw her father walking angrily toward his car.

She watches him get in, slams the door and speeds off. Kiarra was certain that her mother had told him by now. She wondered how she'd ever be able to face him again. Kiarra ran back over to her bed, buried her head in her pillow and began to sob once again. "How could I be so stupid," she thought.

Seeing Through New Eyes

Cleotis opened his eyes. Unsure of where he is, he noticed that the room is extremely bright. "I must have fallen asleep." He thinks as he tries to lift himself into a sitting position. He was caught off guard when he suddenly realized that he couldn't. In fact, he couldn't move at all. His neck is stiff and he tries to look for whatever is restraining him, but his whole body is both numb and tingly at the same time. "Wha….Wha..." He tries to speak but he can't.

"Cleotis," he heard Sally Jame's voice. She seemed to be walking in his direction. When he finally sees her standing over him, he realizes that he is in a bed.

"Wha…Where am I?" Cleotis manages with much effort.

"Shhhh, don't try to talk," Says Sally James, pushing the button to get the nurse's attention.

"You were in a bad car accident Cleotis. You are in the hospital. You've been in a coma for 2 weeks."

"Can I help you?" Cleotis hears a nurse's response to the call for attention.

"Yes, my husband is awake." Sally James says into the speaker.

"I'll inform the doctor."

"Thank you." Says Sally James and then diverts her attention back to Cleotis.

"Everybody has been praying for you, and praise be to God you've finally come to. Cleotis is confused, he tries again to sit up.

"Now, be still Cleotis, the doctor will be in here soon." Obviously anxious, Sally James walked over to the door and looked out to see if the doctor was on the way. Cleotis could not see her, but he could hear her talking with someone outside the door. He felt so tired. He could not help but close his eyes to rest.

Truth Comes to Light

Simone stood in the doorway of the pastor's study, admiring her husband from afar. He had preached a very powerful and anointed sermon today, and she knew that he hadn't quite wound down from it yet. Pastor Parish was startled when he turned to find Simone standing there admiringly in the doorway.

"What is it?" he asks.

"Nothing." She replies.

"Nothing, huh? You're trying to tell me that you're just standing there in the doorway staring at me for the fun of it? Come on Simone…what's on your mind?'

Simone adjusts her feet and looks down at them as she begins to respond. "I was just thinking."

"About what?" Pastor's curiosity had long since been sparked.

"I was just thinking about how lucky I am to be married to such an anointed man of God." She said, crossing her arms as she spoke.

Pastor Parish responded with a smile.

"I mean it, honey," she continued, "you really let God use you today. That sermon spoke to me in so many ways about some things that I have been dealing with lately." Simone walked over and took a seat across from her husband, whose full attention, by now, is on her.

"Oh Baby, that's wonderful, praise God." Pastor Parish reached for his wife's hand.

Simone went on, "That scripture that you took your text from-Psalm 46:10 spoke specifically to me. I mean, I've been all tense and upset lately because I wanted to fix something that isn't even mine to fix."

"What do you mean Simone?"

"Well, first of all, I had to admit to myself that God had not told me to fix anything. Secondly, God also showed me where I hadn't been going about trying to fix things the way that he would have me to. I've been doing things my way and not God's way, and what I got from that passage is that I needed to be still and stop trying to help God out when he doesn't really need my help anyhow. So, I guess I owe you an apology for the way I've been acting lately. I still believe that some things are not the way they should be, but I'm praying, and I know that God's going to work that out too."

Pastor Parish looked at his wife with admiration. He rose from his seat and reached out to draw his wife closer to him. He put his arms gently around her waist and kissed her softly on her lips.

"I'm the one who's lucky," He said.

Simone's attention is captured by the shadow that she sees moving away from the door. Someone had peeked into the office but then quickly dashed away. Startled, Simone moved out of her husband's embrace and toward

71

the door to see who had been there. She catches the back of a woman whom she at first does not recognize.

"Can I help you, Miss?"

Surprised to have been noticed, the woman turned to face her. Simone recognized Ciarra immediately. She recalled having seen her at several of the single's meetings. It was one of the ministries that Simone worked very closely with. Simone realized right away that the woman had been crying.

"Ciarra is your name, right?" Ciarra nodded yes. "You look upset. Is there anything I can do to help?" Simone offered.

"I just need to talk to someone, that's all," Ciarra responded with a little hesitation. "On second thought, maybe I shouldn't have come here. I don't think anyone here can help…. anyway it's my own fault. I should have known better. I don't know how I got into this mess." Simone reached Ciarra a tissue, which she accepted and began using to dab away at the tears streaming down her face.

"Ciarra, why don't you come inside my husband's office for a minute. Maybe the two of us can sit down and talk about this thing. We'll try and make some sense out of whatever has made you so upset…Ok?"

Simone's voice was calm and soothing. She had a knack for knowing just the right way to approach almost any situation. Ciarra took a moment to weigh her options before reluctantly agreeing to go into the office.

"OK." She said as she moved in the direction of the office door.

Simone ushered her into the Pastor's study and with her eyes, signaled Pastor Parish to leave the two of them alone. He caught the hint and exclaimed, "I'll go get the kids from the children's church," as he headed for the door. Simone waited for him to round the corner and then turned her focus to Ciarra, motioning her toward the sofa, where they both took a seat.

"What's wrong, Ciarra?" She asks with genuine concern. She notices that Ciarra seems a little uneasy about whatever it is that she's about to say.

"First Lady Simone, can we please close the door?"

"Sure, honey." Simone rises to go and closes the door.

"I really am not sure that it was right for me to come here. This is my fault too." Ciarra begins looking down at her nervous hands.

"What is your fault?' Simone asks, still unsure of what the problem was.

"I'm pregnant," Ciarra blurts out, bursting into tears. The confession had felt like an explosive going off inside of her. She felt so ashamed she couldn't bear to look Simone in the eyes. She hung her head. Simone reached over to her, and with her soft hands gently stroked Ciarra's cheek and lifted her head so that she could see directly into her eyes. Ciarra was comforted by Simone's warmth and the genuineness of her concern. She was relieved to find that Simone's response to her was not accusative or judgmental.

"Ciarra," Simone began, "I can see why you are upset….and judging by your reaction, I'm assuming that this was not planned. I know that you have your son already, and I'm sure it must be hard being a single parent. Raising children is a difficult task. I couldn't imagine having to do it on my own…."

Ciarra interrupts, "No, you don't really understand yet…. there is more."

Now certain that she did not understand, Simone apologizes, "I'm sorry. I didn't mean to interrupt. Go on Ciarra."

"I'm pregnant by one of the ministers of this church. I don't want to get anybody in trouble or anything, but when I told the father of my baby that I was pregnant, he insisted that it couldn't be his. He told me to have an abortion and said nobody would believe me anyhow if I tried to pin it on him. He's stopped returning my phone calls, and I just don't know what I'm going to do." Ciarra buries her face in her hands and begins to sob again.

"It's alright Ciarra," Simone offers in a comforting tone. "Everything's going to be alright. God will see you through this." Simone wasn't sure what else she could do at this point except reassure her. But there was one thing that she was very certain about. Since this matter involved a minister of the church, her husband would have to be notified. She sat quiet and deep in thought for a while, just trying to offer comfort as best as she could. She thinks to herself, "This is a situation that will have to be handled with extreme care."

Simone begins to speak, "Ciarra, you've told me some pretty heavy stuff. I'm really glad that you found the courage to share this with me. This is not something that you should have to handle alone. I do need to let you know, however, that since what you have told me involves a minister of our church, I will have to share this information with my husband. As Pastor of this church, he has an obligation to handle things of this nature."

"Yes, I understand," Ciarra said. She had gathered herself by now.

"How do you feel about that?" Simone inquired, wanting to be sure that Ciarra was going to be comfortable with what had to be done.

"Well, First Lady Simone. I know that this is not an ideal situation for anyone. But I also feel like I have to be ok with that because you all have to do what you have to do…. So, it has to be done."

"OK, then. I'd like for you to stay here for a moment." Simone said as she moved toward the office door. "I'm going to go and get the Pastor so that you can share with him what you've told me. Make yourself comfortable. There's bottled water in the fridge over there if you'd like some. I'll be right back." Simone pauses, turning toward Ciarra once more before she goes on her way to reassure her. "God's going to work all of this out, Ciarra….don't worry, you'll see."

Simone makes it to the Children's church just as her husband was about to check the kids out.

"Pastor, there is an important matter that needs your attention right away," Simone urges.

Pastor Parish looks at her with confusion, "What's going on, Simone?" He asks.

"Leave the kids here for a while longer, you're needed in your office right away. It will all be explained when we get there." Taking her husband by the hand, she leads him away offering no additional information. As they leave, Simone beckons to inform the caregiver that they will return for the children shortly. The two walk briskly back down the hallway to the Pastor's study. They find Ciarra seated on the sofa, dabbing at her eyes with a tissue as they enter the room. Pastor Parish could tell by the anxious look on the woman's face that something is very much wrong. Simone takes a seat on the sofa beside Ciarra and places her arm around her shoulder for support.

"Ciarra," She begins slowly, "The Pastor needs to know what you have shared with me."

"Ok," Ciarra replies nervously, her eyes dancing about back and forward from the Pastor to his wife. "This is really embarrassing…I'm so ashamed." She blurts out, looking toward the sky. Pastor Parish walks over to where she is sitting and kneels next to her. He looks into her eyes and says with sincerity, "Sister Porter, I am only human. I make mistakes too, we all do. For that reason, I can't judge you. Only God can do that, and he already knows. There's no reason to be ashamed to tell me, Ok.

"Ok," Ciarra responds, nodding her head to indicate that she did.

"Now, tell me what's wrong." Pastor Parish's voice is filled with concern. Ciarra begins to tell him what she'd previously shared with Simone. Pastor Parish listened intently. He was very dismayed at what he was hearing. He didn't understand how this could happen. He also wondered which of his ministers would do such a thing. He listened on until Ciarra had finished. A million thoughts were running through his mind. When he was finally able to speak, he asked, "Who is this minister that you have been involved with?"

Ciarra looked down at her feet. She doesn't want to disclose the name of her baby's father, but she knows that it has to be done. Simone, who is sitting nearby, senses her hesitation and reassures her that she is doing the right thing.

"It's Rev. Magee, Pastor. He is the father of my baby." Ciarra looked through her tear clouded eyes directly into the Pastor's eyes where she hoped to find some reassurance that she was doing the right thing. What she saw appeared to be shock, which then quickly turned into concern once he was able to gather himself.

Although he tried his best to conceal it, what this woman had just disclosed had hit Pastor Parish hard. Julius had always been a ladies' man, but Pastor Parish had never thought much of that. After all, he was single. So, Pastor Parish had never thought that there was anything wrong with his friend engaging in a little harmless flirtation. However, never in a million years would he have expected anything this extreme…especially involving a member of the church. All he could think was, "What has Julius done? Is he crazy! He knows better than this!" Pastor Parish finds himself at a loss for words. He looks over at his wife for support.

Simone, who senses his shock and hesitation, begins to speak for him.

"Ciarra, I know it must have been extremely hard for you to come forth with this. We really appreciate your trusting us enough to be able to come to us with this very sensitive situation. This is very serious, and I assure you that this will be dealt with in a confidential and sensitive manner."

Pastor Parish, who had finally managed to regroup, nods his appreciation to Simone and then finds his words.

He starts to speak. "Miss Porter, I wish that I knew a quick and easy way to fix this, but I don't. As my wife said this matter will be handled with care, and I want you to know that we will support you and help you through this situation in any way that we can. Please feel free to call on us for anything that you might need."

Ciarra is comforted by his words. She nods her head in response.

"Miss Porter," he continues in a very serious tone, "I need to know if you'd feel comfortable agreeing to meet with me, my wife, and Rev. Magee sometime soon?" He goes on to explain. "This would help so that we could all sit down, discuss this matter and come to some appropriate conclusions about how this can best be handled." He pauses momentarily. "I know that this might be difficult for you, but will you agree to meet with us?"

"Yes, Pastor," Ciarra responds. "You're right this will be hard, but I have to assume some responsibility for what has happened too. I made a mistake, and I know this won't be easy. But I'm willing to do what I have to do to make things right for everyone involved. Especially this child," she exclaimed, looking down at her still unassuming belly. "Just let me know when, and I'll be here. I prayed about this situation all night, and now after talking to you all, I know I'm doing the right thing."

"You certainly are." Offered Simone rising from the sofa with Ciarra and gently holding her hand as she escorted her to the door. She extended her arms to offer a hug. "God's gonna make this alright, Ciarra, you'll see." She stated in a most uplifting tone. "The Bible tells us that He would never leave us or forsake us. He promises to be there for us when we need Him, so you just trust Him, OK…." She released Ciarra from her embrace and added. "Please call me if you need anything, alright?"

"Alright," Ciarra replies before turning to exit the door. "Thanks again to both of you for your help. It really means a lot."

Simone watches as Ciarra walks down the hall. She is suddenly overtaken by exhaustion. She turns around to face her husband, whose expression is one of total disbelief. At that moment, she felt sorry for him. She had been suspicious of Julius's dealings with women in the church for quite some time, but not even she had wanted to believe the things she had just heard. She was sure that this had totally caught her husband off guard. She also knew that this situation was going to require her to be both prayerful and supportive of him. For some time now, she had been trying to get her husband to look past his friendship with Julius and see the truth. But her husband had refused. Part of her felt good that Julius's mess had finally surfaced and come to light, but the other part of her felt bad for her husband. She knew how devoted he was to his friend. He trusted him. So, she could only imagine how painful dealing with this was going to be for him. She watched as her husband picked up the phone and began dialing. He was calling Julius.

"Hey, Ju…" he paused as though the words were hard to get out, "I need to talk to you, man. I need you to come to the church and meet with me right now." Pastor Parish did not wait for a reply. He hung up the phone, placed it back on the receiver, and then turned to face Simone. It was difficult to see such pain in his eyes. She walks over to her husband and puts her arms around him.

"Simone," He said, looking into her eyes as he spoke, "I'm sorry."

"You don't need to apologize…." She responded. "That is your friend, and you trusted him."

"Yes, I do." He interrupts. "You tried to warn me, but I didn't want to listen. For that…. I'm sorry…."

Simone allows him to continue, "I'm going to have to talk with Julius today." He hesitated. "And when I'm done here…. You and I are going to need to talk about something when I get home. I'm so sorry…."

"Really honey, it's Ok. You don't need to keep apologizing…" Simone offers comfort and insists that he did not need to say more. But he insists and continues on.

"You don't understand, Simone. I do need to apologize. There are some things that you don't know. We have a lot to talk about. But I've got to deal with this first. Right now, I just need you to go home and wait for me there, OK."

Simone is confused, but seeing how serious and troubled her husband already was, she wants to do what she can to support him. "OK honey," she relents, "I'll go wait for you at home. I love you." With that, she kisses him on the cheek and heads for the door. She said a silent prayer for him as she and her kids made their way out to the car. Just as she is leaving, she sees Julius pulling up. She watches as he parks his red convertible and checks his hair in the rear-view mirror before getting out and heading up the walkway into the church. "God, please give my husband the strength that he needs." She thinks to herself and then drives away.

Pray One for Another

The doorbell rings. Sis Bebe opens the door to find Kiara's best friend, Kelly standing there. "Yes?" She says in an agitated voice.

"Hi, Mrs. Smith. I just came by to see Kiarra and to find out how she's doing. I haven't talked to her in a while, and I just wanted to make sure that she is OK. I've been calling, but she hasn't been returning any of my messages."

Sis BeBe interrupted abruptly. "That's cuz I haven't been giving her any of your messages. It's hanging out with fast girls like you that got her into trouble in the first place. You just ain't got caught up with yet."

Kelly is caught off guard by Sis. Bebe's accusations. She feels a heated sensation going all throughout her body, and her eyes start to tear up as she searches for her words.

"Mrs. Smith, I'm not a fast girl…" tears start to roll down her face, she had tried to hold them back but had not been able to "It embarrasses me that you would even think that way about me. I'm a virgin, and I've made a pledge to God that I will remain that way until I am married." Kelly turns to walk away but stops at the sound of Kiarra's voice calling her name.

"Kelly, please don't go." Begs Kiarra moving past her mother to open the screen door and motioning to invite her in. Kiarra had witnessed the entire conversation and was angered by the way that her mother had treated her friend. "How could you say those things to her???!! She didn't do anything wrong. It was all me! Me! Me! Me! I'm the one who got pregnant! Not her! And you have not said one word to me about it! Do you have anything to say about that mom???" Kiarra's obvious irritation with her mother puts her on edge.

Be Be looks around to see if anyone is watching. "Kiarra, lower your voice before the neighbors hear you and wonder what's going on." She snaps impatiently. This causes Kiarra's annoyance to grow. "Why do you always care so much about what everybody else thinks? What about me???! Don't I matter?? What about what I think???!"

Sis. Be Be becomes impatient as she notices the people passing by are starting to stare. She waves and throws a fake smile in their direction. She is clearly agitated as she begins speaking under her breath to her daughter. "How dare you raise your voice to me like that Kiarra, your daddy and me have always given you everything you wanted…. sometimes before you could even ask for it…."

"Maybe that's the problem…" Kiarra interrupts to reply. "You and daddy give me everything I want…. everything money can buy. You let me do what I want. You never tell me no. But you've never given me what I really need. I need guidance! I need love! I need your time. What about those things' mom? Aren't they important too?…….You and daddy have always been so busy with work, church, this organization, that organization, or another. You've never had time for me, mom. I need you and daddy to be my parents and just pay attention to me sometimes." Kiarra turns to her friend Kelly for comfort as her emotions take over and she begins to sob. Kelly embraces her friend and tries to console her. Overcome by her own emotions and the realization of the truth that her daughter has just spoken, Be Be goes over to where the girls are standing and reaches for her daughter.

"I'm so sorry baby. I didn't know. I'm so sorry." She exclaims through her sobs as the two of them hold each other in a tight embrace until they can cry no more. Kiarra's friend Kelly stands by, looking on for a few minutes before she turns to leave. "As beautiful as this is, this is a sacred and private moment." She thinks to herself. The mother and daughter, still lost in the moment, do not notice as she exits the door. Kelly praises God on her way down the steps for helping her friend and marveled at how wonderful God truly is. This is what she had prayed for all along. He had answered her prayer, and she was ecstatic that He had helped her friend.

The Truth Shall Set You Free

Simone rushes to peek out the window. She thought she'd heard a car door close outside. She had been anxiously waiting near the window, running to peek at every sound she heard outside for the last few minutes. She had made it home from church and put the kids to bed. It had been over 3 hours by now, and she hadn't expected that it would take her husband so long to get home. She thought about calling to make sure everything was OK. But she didn't want to add any excess anxiety to what he was already feeling. She wanted to be a support. He'd asked her to go and wait for him at home, so that was what she needed to do. However, it was hard just waiting idly by, and time seemed to be creeping. So, she prayed for God to make everything alright, and she waited. She looked out the window once more and saw her husband just as he was bending to retrieve his briefcase from the backseat. "I need to see his face," she thinks, "then I can know that everything is alright." But, as he turns to walk toward the house she observes, instead, a look of complete heaviness. The Holy Spirit quickens her, and these words come to her mind, "for the spirit of heaviness put on the garment of praise."

"Satan, the blood of Jesus is against you," she states authoritatively. "I rebuke you in the name of Jesus….and I praise God, for you will not steal my joy today." Simone rushes to the front door and turns the knob to open the door and greet her husband. She throws her arms around him and says, "Praise the Lord! I'm so glad you're finally home." She lets go of her embrace and reaches to take his briefcase. Then, she helps him remove his jacket and places it in the coat closet. She guides him into the family room and motions for him to sit on the sofa. She notices that her husband appears defeated and heavy as he willingly complies with her demands.

"Let me put these things away, and I'll get you something to drink. I'll be right back." Simone says nervously.

"Simone," Pastor Parish says. You can tell by his tone that he is exhausted. "I have something very important to tell you, and I just need for you to listen."

"Oh, I will," Simone interrupts, "but let me get you something to drink first."

"NO SIMONE!" His tone is harsh, and it startles Simone. Pastor Parish realizes it and immediately apologizes. He rises from the sofa, motions for his wife's hand and gently pulls her over to the sofa to be seated next to him. "I'm sorry baby. I didn't mean to yell. I just need to tell you something that is going to be very hard. I've been praying all evening that God will help me to do this. But……"

"What is it honey?" Simone could tell by the look in his eyes that this was serious.

"Simone….it happened a long time ago…." he pauses before continuing on, "I got a woman pregnant."

Simone's mouth drops open as she is shocked and speechless at this revelation. Uncomfortable with the silence that follows what he had just revealed, and unsure of how his wife's reaction can be interpreted, Pastor Parish continues to explain. "You and I had been married for a year Simone, and as you may remember, that was a tough year. We had a lot of problems, and we argued a lot. You knew God, but at that time I didn't. You kept pushing me and challenging me…. and I just didn't think that I was gonna be able to live up to your expectations. I was so young and immature. One night after we had gotten into an argument, Julius and I went out to this club…." Simone sits motionlessly as she quietly listens for him to continue. She is still puzzled at what she has just heard. She can't help but to wish that this is all a bad dream so that can just pinch herself and wake up. But there is no escaping what she just heard, and the words her husband speaksas he continues. "There were these two women who were at the club together that night. Julius started talking to one of them, and I started talking to the other. We had some drinks, one thing led to another, and before you know it…. we were all at a hotel." He stops. The rest was just too hard to say.

"Go on." Simone's voice is ice as she insists that he continues.

"Well, you know the rest." Pastor Parish says, looking down at his hands.

"I want to hear you say it." Simone's voice is firm.

Reluctantly, he continues. "I slept with her……I slept with her, and she became pregnant. Once I found out, I told her I was married but that I would take care of the baby. She agreed not to try and cause any problems with my marriage if I did what I said. She carried the baby for 5 months, and then she had a miscarriage. I didn't tell anybody else about it but Julius. .... I couldn't tell you. I was too afraid that you'd leave me...." As difficult as it was, he looked into Simone's eyes. "I didn't want you to leave me, Simone. I realized my mistake. It was stupid, and I was so ashamed...but I knew I couldn't live without you."

Tears began to weld up in his eyes. Simone sits quiet and motionless for what seem like forever to him. She was not sure of her feelings or what to say. So, in that moment she just watches him sob, as his eyes plead with her for forgiveness.

"Why are you telling me this now?" She asks calmly. She's not able to offer him comfort.

"Julius has always been my best friend. But the truth is, he's never liked my being with you.... always said you changed me. We vowed to keep what happened between us. I figured, knowing Julius, though, that if I ever made him mad, he'd be more than glad to tell you about what happened in the hopes that it would break us up so that he and I could be like we used to be."

Simone tries to digest all that she has just heard. It suddenly made sense to her why her husband had always seemed to turn a blind eye whenever Julius did something wrong. It wasn't right....and probably a little selfish on his part.... but he was acting out of the fear of losing her.

"Simone," Pastor Parish begins to plead, "I promise you that I have never even thought about touching another woman since then. I love you Simone and I pray to God every day that you will be able to forgive me."

Simone sighs, "I know you love me, but this is all very hard to hear. …I love you too. More than anything on this earth. This is not going to be easy. This is gonna take some time to process…and a lot of prayer. But I trust God, and I know that he is able to see us through even this. God's will be done." With that, Simone wipes away his tears and then pulls him closer to her. He lays his head on her soft breasts, and places his arms around her waist. She willingly accepts his embrace as she caresses the back of his head and neck ever so gently.

When Our Eyes Are Opened

Deacon Douglass had been driving for quite a while. After work, he'd meant to go to a bar and get a drink or two before going home to all the gloom and doom that he knew would be awaiting him there. But somehow, he'd ended up just driving around with no particular destination in mind. He looked at his watch. To his surprise, he'd been driving for over two hours.

"Maybe I should give Betty Jean a call," he thinks to himself. Betty Jean always knew how to make him feel good. But, on the other hand, Betty Jean came with a cost, and Deacon Douglass really wasn't in the mood to deal with her and all her wants today. Ever since he'd found out about his little girl getting pregnant, he just hadn't felt right. The realization that he'd agreed with his wife, BeBe to make his daughter have an abortion because of what people might think made him feel even worse. It was all just too much for him. He'd argued with BeBe several times regarding what the Bible says about killing and life. But, eventually he had gone against what he believed so strongly and had given in to Be Be's desires. However, now he has come to fully regret his decision. He had acted to save his own face, instead of out of obedience to God. He started thinking that maybe this was God's way of punishing him for some of the things he had done.

"This whole thing is my fault." Deacon Douglass mumbles aloud. "The Bible lets us know that fornication, adultery, taking a life, and dishonoring your family are wrong……and here I've been doing it all. It seemed like

I'd been getting away with it, but I hadn't really. Look at what's happened to my baby! My own child has had to suffer because of my mess. While I was out doing what I was doing, I should have been there for her. Maybe then none of this would have happened...."

Tears begin to flow uncontrollably down Deacon Douglass's face making it hard for him to see where he is going. He pulls the car over to the side of the road. Throws his hands up toward the heavens and through his tears exclaims, "Oh God......I know I've done wrong.... Please forgive me Lord.......please forgive me Lord....."

The Final Say

"ALRIGHT EVERYONE! IF YOU WILL PLEASE COME TO ORDER IT IS TIME TO BEGIN OUR BOARD MEETING. EVERYBODY QUIET DOWN PLEASE."

Pastor Parish arises from his seat, taking the floor as he begins to speak. "Thank you Deacon Douglass for calling everyone to order." He pauses for a moment and looks upward as though he is searching the air for the words that he was about to say. Pastor Parish's solemn mood and the extended silence that he allowed for a seemingly lengthy amount of time puts everyone on edge as they quietly wait. The silence is thick. Finally, he speaks. "Let us pray before we begin." Pastor Parish prays that the board meeting will be held in a professional manner, but most importantly that he follows God's lead in addressing the decisions and changes that were about to take place. He prays that honesty, repentance, and compassion will take place and that anger and conviction will not rule in their midst. He asks God's forgiveness for falling short of being the leader that he was called to be, and he asks God for another chance. He prays for the strength and the wisdom to be able to do all that God desires of him, and then concludes his prayer with "in the name of Jesus, Amen."

Before he began to address the board committee, Pastor Parish glanced in his wife's direction. Their eyes meet only briefly, but in that second, he finds in her eyes the encouragement that he needs to go on.

92

"Ladies and gentlemen," he begins, "I'm so glad that you could make it out this evening. I know you could have been somewhere else, but I appreciate your coming here. There are several important things that need to be discussed and handled amongst our church family members today." The committee members sit quietly, looking on with curiosity as he continues. "I must tell you that I feel kind of heavy this evening.... because some of these things that we have to deal with are unpleasant......and I can't help but to feel somewhat responsible. God made me your leader, and He called me to be a good Shepherd of this house. I know that along with the title comes the responsibility of leading the flock in the way of the Lord. It is my duty to keep you all covered and protected.... But I've failed some of you, and in failing some of you, I've failed us all. The whole family. Some people have been harmed by the leadership of this church. Leaders are supposed to be working for the good of the church, but in our case, some of our leaders have instead been taking advantage of hurting members of the church." Pastor Parish looks out amongst the committee members to observe their reactions, but more importantly to make sure that he still has their attention. He finds that all eyes are indeed focused on him, so he continues. "Some of you might say it's not my fault, because I'm not responsible for the actions of others, but I say to you that I take full ownership for some of the things that have gone wrong, because I am the one who chose each of our leaders for their positions. The problem is, I chose without inquiring of the Lord ... .and because of this, some people have unfortunately been hurt." The room went silent. No one was exactly sure of what

Pastor Parish was referring to or where his thoughts were headed, but by now, everyone was waiting with bated breath for what he'd say next. He went on, "I suppose now that you are all wondering what I am talking about. Well, for starters, Pastor Magee has been removed from the position of Co-Pastor due to the fact that he has impregnated one of our single members and because of other reports of offenses that are of a sexual nature involving various female members of the church." For a moment, it felt as though everyone in the room had released a sigh of surprise at the very same time.

Pastor Parish, finding it hard to have just spoken those words, paused for a moment to catch his breath. The words had not been easy for him to say, but even so, he felt as though a load had been lifted from his entire being, and he knew that addressing the rest of his concerns would be much easier. Members of the congregation looked on in confusion and disbelief as he continued. "In addition, we've recently found out that our head minister of music has been charged with child molestation. "Pastor Parish states sorrowfully, shaking his head in disbelief. "He has apparently been engaging in sexual misconduct with some of our young girls."

The noise level rises, as comments of obvious disdain and disapproval are expressed by members throughout the building.

Pastor Parish continues, "The police have been looking for him but have gotten reports from his mother saying that he's left town, and she doesn't know where to find him. His poor mother, whom as many of you know, is disabled, has had to be put in an elderly home." More gasps and comments of shock and disapproval are expressed among members of the committee.

Pastor Parish pauses again briefly, before he continues on. When he starts to speak again, tears begin to form in his eyes. "I just feel so responsible for all of this," he adds, "these things never should have happened......and I've prayed and asked God for forgiveness because I know that I have not been the man or leader that he has called me to be. I have let you all down....and I am sorry." Pastor Parish moves slowly toward his seat, his head hung low and with tears streaming down his face. Simone reaches to embrace her husband as he approaches his seat. "You did the right thing, honey, and God is pleased." She reassures.

One of the older members of the board speaks out with obvious displeasure about what has just been said. "I'll bet poor Rev. Magee Senior is just rolling over in his grave at all this mess going on in his church. He would have never let anything like this happen if he would have still been here, God rest his soul." A few heads nod in agreement while some others offer 'amens'. But suddenly, from out of nowhere, a loud unfamiliar voice speaks up from the back of the sanctuary. Everyone turns their head in the direction the voice is coming from.

"That's a lie!" The voice moves closer toward the front of the room. "That's a lie, and you all know it." It was Cleotis James. A sudden wave of surprise swept over the committee, and looks of disdain overpowered the facial expressions of many of the board members... including his wife's. Sis. Sally James looked on in disbelief, not sure how to react at this point. She couldn't believe that Cleotis would be interrupting the board meeting and speaking out so boldly like this. As a board member, she had been required to attend the meeting, but Cleotis was only there to clean the church and get it ready for Sunday service. Since they had driven to the church together, she was certain that he had not been drinking. Aside from that, Cleotis had been like a new person since his car accident, and she was never really sure what to expect from him anymore.

From the back of the church, Cleotis walked confidently down the aisle between the center pews. When he reached the front of the church, he stopped and turned to face the committee members who were in attendance. All eyes were focused on him as they were all still shocked to see him standing there… with a broom in his hands, but obviously about to make a statement. "What is he doing? Is he drunk?" A few whispers and snickers permeate the silence as everyone looks on, waiting to see what's about to happen. Cleotis clears his throat, first nodding toward the pastor and his wife as a show of respect and then boldly glancing over the entire audience before he begins to speak.

"I know y'all are all wondering what I'm doing up here. I can see it on your faces…. some of y'all are sitting in your seats right now judging me cause you figure I'm just an old drunk who ain't got no business trying to tell nobody nothing. Well…. It's true that I was a drunk once upon a time, but that's changed…. And if the truth be told, most all of you out there have been somebody or done something ungodly at one point or another during your own lives. But the thing is… you sit out there like you got the right to judge me, or like you can judge the Pastor over there for our shortcomings… because maybe you think your sins are smaller than ours. The Bible says that we All have sinned and come short of the Glory of God. I've been cleaning this church for years, and I've seen a lot of things going on. I've seen some of you coming in here day in and day out working in the church and shouting harder than anybody… and then I've also seen many of you leaving this church house and just living any old kind of way out there in the world when you think no one is watching. Some of you don't even wait until you get out of the church house to do your business. But God sees us everywhere we go. So, he knows that I've been a drunk most of my life…. Sometimes I've drank for my own pleasure, but there have been other times when I've drank to try and cope with making some sense of all these things that I've seen going on inside and outside of this church. Things I couldn't tell nobody, because drunks don't get much respect, you know…. And nobody would have believed me. The same kinds of things that I've seen going on around here lately have been going on here for years. It's just happening with different folks now. What I've learned, though, is that in the eyes of God, all of our sins are equal. Another thing that I have learned is that God knew and cared about all those things I kept inside and tried to drink away. I didn't realize it before because I was too drunk to acknowledge him, but he was there listening to me when I told him about all that I saw all the time. Often, he spoke to me and told me to tell his people that he was not pleased. But, I kept hiding behind my alcohol, fearing that nobody would listen to me anyway…. because who was I to tell somebody what God said? The truth is, I was ashamed of myself….and I just didn't see how God could use somebody like me. Until God saved my life and gave me another chance. I almost died in that car accident I had back here a while ago. I promised the Lord if he'd let me live, I'd live for him and do what's right……and that's exactly what I intend to do. I'm starting right now Pastor by letting you know that you were right to assume responsibility for the shortcomings of the leaders of your flock. But what you need to do now is put aside your worry about what the rest of these people in here think, and accept that God has forgiven you. You go and be the man, the leader… that God has called you to be. Pastor you've got God and a beautiful, wise, and spirit filled wife by your side. With a combination like that, you gone be alright." Cleotis turned to address Simone. "First Lady, I want to thank you for always treating me with respect, even when I probably didn't deserve it."

"God bless you." Simone mouthed silently from where she was seated.

"I also need to say one last thanks to my wife. I never really appreciated her like I should have before, but since my accident, she has been right there by my side nursing me back to health. In a way, as bad as my accident seemed when I was going through it all…. I think it may have been the best thing that could have happened to me…or that could have ever happened to us. God has opened my eyes and given me a new revelation. If ya'll don't mind, I'd like to share with you a little poem that God gave me a long time ago. I encourage you to take it for whatever it speaks to you. It goes like this….

God is not pleased with my ugly ways

When I clap my hands, sing his songs of praise

When I shout 'hallelujah' at just the right time

When I testify that victory is mine

When no sooner have I left the church yard

Do I take off my mask and let down my guard

I'll go home and cuss my old woman out

Fuss at my children and shove them about

Then I'll call Bro. Thomas on the phone

To see if he saw what Sis. Sarah had on

I'll sit in my lounge chair, my heels all kicked up

And sip on the liquor I poured in my cup

My religion I've boxed up and stuck on a shelf

Until further notice or until I need help

But on Sunday, I will take it back out again

Without ever having acknowledged my sin

You'll find me sitting on the front church pew

The same old thing is what I will do

NO....God is not pleased with my ugly ways.

The church was silent. To Cleotis, it felt like the silence lasted forever. Unsure of how the committee had received what he had just shared, he nervously began to make his way down the center aisle toward the back door of the church. He didn't notice at first, but several members of the committee had stood to their feet and began to applaud. Before he could reach the back door, the applause was overwhelming and could not be ignored. Everyone in the room was standing. The presence of God could be felt all around. A few of the members could be heard giving praises to the Lord. The Holy Spirit had taken over, and a few of the committee members had begun to shout. Cleotis's testimony had been touching. Praise began to break out all across the sanctuary. Sis. Sally James walked out into the center aisle, where she met Cleotis. She threw her arms around him. She was beaming with pride.

"Cleotis," she said, "I am so proud of you. I had no idea that you could write like that."

Cleotis looked into her eyes and responded. "To tell you the truth, Sally left on my own, and I can't. But with the help of God, I can do all things just as the Bible says.... And sometimes, I'm even surprised at what I come up with myself. I'll tell you the truth baby, God is some kind of good...."

Milton Keynes UK
Ingram Content Group UK Ltd.
UKHW021919151124
451262UK00014B/1501

9 798330 544202